"Why did you betray me?"

Blaine looked almost savage, those hard hands balled into fists in an effort not to touch Lydia.

"First you say it wasn't for the money," he continued. "Now you're telling me it wasn't for another man. Then why did you leave me?"

"I didn't love you." The lie burned Lydia's throat like acid. She gave a small cry as his arms locked around her.

"Liar! You were as hopelessly out of control as I was...as I am now...."

ELIZABETH POWER was born in Bristol, England, where she lives with her husband, in a three-hundred-year-old cottage. A keen reader, she had already, as a teenager, made up her mind to be a novelist, although it wasn't until around the age of thirty that she took up writing seriously. Elizabeth is an animal lover, with a strong leaning toward vegetarianism. Her interests include organic vegetable gardening, regular exercise, listening to music, fashion and ministering to the demands of her adopted, generously proportioned cat!

The Wedding Betrayal

ELIZABETH POWER

DARK SECRETS

HARLEQUIN®

TORONTO • NEW YORK • LONDON
AMSTERDAM • PARIS • SYDNEY • HAMBURG
STOCKHOLM • ATHENS • TOKYO • MILAN • MADRID
PRAGUE • WARSAW • BUDAPEST • AUCKLAND

ISBN 0-373-80541-1

THE WEDDING BETRAYAL

First North American Publication 2001.

Copyright © 1999 by Elizabeth Power.

Visit us at www.eHarlequin.com

Printed in U.S.A.

CHAPTER ONE

A MAID had shown her in.

The magnificent room, with its fine antiques and classic furnishings, offered up a view of floodlit water and a curved verandah beyond the long glass doors, and there was a slight compression to Lydia's soft, perfect mouth that said she hadn't failed to be impressed.

The house—or rather waterfront estate!—*was* impressive, even for one who once, in another life, it seemed, had seen and touched the playgrounds of the mega-rich.

The doors were open to the July night, and the scent of some exotic shrub drifted in, causing her nostrils to dilate, her jet-lag to diminish in the sweet humidity.

Three weeks in Bermuda was just what she needed, even if it did include looking after somebody else's twelve-year-old son, and she was grateful to Heather for telling her about it, suggesting that she take the job herself.

Approaching footsteps made her turn on the exquisitely patterned rug, the smile that came so effortlessly to her lips fading with the instant recognition of the man who strode into the room.

Tall and dark, and yet more imposing even than she remembered, his strong features were turning bloodless from the shock that only seemed to mirror her own.

'You!' There was shock, too, in the rasped monosyllable that escaped from between those grim masculine lips, from a mouth that had been hardened by the years.

Like those cold grey eyes that were scored now by deep laughter lines. And not only laughter, she suspected, from the look of him, because there was a harshness to Blaine Caldwell's maturity that was redeemed from the tyrannical only by his dark attraction, by that smouldering sensuality which, she despaired to realise at once, he still possessed.

'Blaine!'

'What the hell are you doing here?' His voice was rough against the chirruping of crickets, his eyes demanding as they raked over the perfect structure of her face with its full, wide mouth and Slavic cheekbones, over the chic, short hairstyle that had long since replaced the heavy dark mane of silken waves.

'Someone wanted a nanny…' She couldn't quite control the tremor in her voice, her thoughts swirling like a turbulent river. What must she look like to him? she wondered hectically. She'd be thirty-two this year! Not the eighteen-year-old model to whom he had proposed in a frenzy of desire. 'Someone by the name of Thornton.' Not Blaine Caldwell! She only hoped it was true when everyone said she still looked only twenty-five!

'That's right. Dale Thornton. My associate.' He strode further into the room now, slipping his hands into the pockets of his light, well tailored trousers. 'He flew Liam out here.'

There was a little sprinkling of grey in the once jet-black hair at his temples, Lydia was relieved to notice, hardly taking in what he was saying. But time had been kind to him, she could scarcely deny, because he was still powerfully lean beneath the short-sleeved casual shirt and slacks he wore—as he had always worn his clothes—with a head-turning elegance that had only improved with the years. So much so that in her sleeveless white blouse and loose-fitting beige slacks she had chosen for the journey, she felt rather drab and dishevelled beside him.

Awareness, however, flared in her as vitally as it had ever done, leaving her throat constricted on a wave of something closely akin to fear.

'It was Thornton who arranged things with the agency,' she heard him telling her.

'Then...' A thin line creased her forehead. 'This Liam's *your* son?'

'Right again.' He came to stand, long legs planted firmly astride on the expensive rug, just in front of her. 'And you're telling me you didn't know that?'

His inexorable grimness told her he didn't believe her. But she hadn't known.

'No, I—' She broke off, puzzled. Had Heather?

'Doesn't that agency you work for tell you anything?' His tone was brusque, irate.

'Heather took the details.' She lifted her gaze from the light masculine shoes she hadn't realised she had been staring at. 'And she and I are partners,' she went on to enlighten him firmly, her eyes challenging, her shoulders squared.

'You co-own...' Astonishment tinged his voice. 'What was it called?' He fished around for the name of the London agency that she and her friend had started together four years ago. 'Caring Days?' The initial surprise in his face was replaced by a scornful smile. 'And when did you suddenly begin to learn to care, Lydia?'

Though he couldn't have known, she felt his contempt like the cutting edge of a knife.

'It's all been a mistake. I'm sorry.' Slipping the strap of the bag she'd discarded on a chair over her shoulder, she made a sudden, hurried move towards the door.

'You're going?'

That harsh accusation made her stop, caused her slim shoulders to tense from a myriad of emotions.

'Walking out? Just like you did before?'

She swung round now, the guarded sapphire of her eyes concealing a depth of pain at which he could never begin to guess.

'That's all in the past.' The weighty feeling in her chest made it difficult to speak. 'I think I'd better go.'

'Why?' He started towards her, his hands at his sides, every inch of him condemning. 'Isn't the price high enough this time?'

Her chin came up, exposing her pale throat and the fine symmetry of features made famous by the camera that had loved her.

'I never had a price, Blaine,' she whispered, her voice controlled.

'No?' he said with a sceptical lift of an eyebrow, and he laughed now in brutal mockery. 'Just how big a cheque did it take from my father to buy you off?'

Her eyelids drooped at the memory, the dark smudges under her eyes caused by more than just jet-lag and fatigue.

It was best that he hated her. 'Best for everyone that you just disappear,' Henry Caldwell had assured her in that soft, pitiless voice all those years ago, rather than let his son—and everyone else—know the truth about her.

'I'll get you a replacement.' Determinedly she turned away again, saying, 'It should only take a day or two.'

'Yes, it's easy to walk away, isn't it?' Strong fingers, burning on her bare arm, pulled her round to face him, making her senses reel from the sudden shock of his closeness. 'How many times have you done it since? Or are your younger charges less of a threat to your glorious freedom?'

In a daze of turbulent emotion she realised that he had already noticed she wasn't wearing a ring. But the harsh reality of him after all these years revived the torture of feelings she had been forced to repress, and now she sobbed on a little note of alarm, 'Let me go!'

That intelligent brow furrowed as he studied the tense beauty of her features, and perhaps he misconstrued the reason for the fear in her eyes because he complied, abruptly releasing her.

'I'm sorry.' He raked his fingers through his thick dark hair and for a moment the deep grooves scoring his face made him look every bit what he was: a man nearing forty. 'I've no intention of hurting you, though God knows there were times when I would dearly have loved to!'

Were there? Had he really wanted to hurt her? she wondered, catching that strange note of intensity in his voice. Had her seemingly cruel betrayal touched him in ways that had never been apparent?

'You didn't mourn me for long?' She was glad, in a way, that he hadn't, though in others she had known such severity of pain that she had wanted to die when he had married Sharon Hillier only two months after their own break-up.

'No.' There. It was an admission. What more could she want than that? He had filled the void with the lovely redhead and a child, while she had been alone and tortured, tortured by the agonies of hell!

'Liam needs someone *now*.' That deep voice cut harshly through her thoughts. 'From tomorrow. I can't get anyone else over here in time without disrupting a very important schedule. Your agency promised unreservedly that they'd get someone here in time to meet my requirements.'

His requirements. Not his and Sharon's—because his beautiful socialite wife had been killed when her car had hit a tree outside their London home eighteen months ago. Lydia couldn't even remember now who had told her that.

'What the hell are you doing playing nursemaid anyway? It doesn't exactly go hand in hand with my memories of the lovely Lydia Lawrence. Did the good life finally pale—even for you?'

His contempt was flaying, but she chose to ignore it.

'And what are you doing here if—as you say—you co-own the blasted business? Or was the thought of Bermuda too much of a temptation?'

He was giving her no quarter, and, in his eyes at least, she decided, she probably didn't deserve any.

'Something like that,' she admitted, and thought, Well, it had been, hadn't it? 'I'd been overworking.' She hated telling him that. It gave her a vulnerability she didn't want to show to him. And not because she feared him, so much as herself. 'I'd been forced to take a few weeks off,' she continued as prosaically as she could. 'I missed a holiday last year. And Heather rang me with the details of this job that had come through.' But she hadn't told her everything, Lydia was sure. 'I won't leave you in the lurch.'

The sound that escaped Blaine was derisory, before he said, 'That'll be an all-time first.'

She ignored that, too.

'I'll look after Liam for you,' she told him steadfastly. 'At least until we can get a replacement who can take over from me. That is…if you want me to.'

Sapphire eyes, dark with a hidden torment, lifted and her gaze locked with the icy silver of his.

She wanted him to say that no, that wouldn't do. That he didn't want her in his house, because all *she* wanted to do was to get away from there, jump in a taxi and take the merciful journey to the nearest hotel.

He didn't say that at all, however, but merely asked, 'You think you're up to it?'

Lydia's forehead puckered. Did she look that fragile?

'My flight was delayed for nearly three hours. I had a lot of waiting around,' she explained unnecessarily. He must have checked the time of her flight before he'd sent that chauffeur-driven limousine to meet her. 'Anyway, I'd completed my sickness leave,' she went on with positive assurance. 'I would have been back at work tomorrow morning.'

A muscle pulled in Blaine's jaw before he strode over to press a bell beside the large, traditionally English stone fireplace.

'I'm ordering some coffee. Would you like some?'

His assessing glance over her sleek, slim figure opened up a cache of bittersweet memories. The way those eyes smouldered with an awareness of her that even after all these years hadn't been totally extinguished; that proud way he carried himself—like a sleek, predatory cat…

She shook her head. 'I never drink the stuff.'

'Ah, no…I remember.'

Did he?

'Tea always, wasn't it?'

She nodded, and with a silent agony prayed, Please don't remember anything else. I couldn't bear it! Oh, God! Why was she agreeing to spend even an hour in this house?

'And what spurred you to make the transition from super-model to super-nanny, Lydia? Somehow the two don't seem to go hand in hand.'

A nervous breakdown! The need to become anonymous! To go into hiding, she heard her heart screaming, but said only, 'I've had all the necessary training. I can show you my qualifications if you're in any doubt.'

He smiled, a mere movement of lips that did nothing to warm his eyes as he came back to her.

'Now why would you imagine I could ever doubt anything you say?'

Because that was what he'd presumed she was when she had thrown him over, supposedly for another man and after only the briefest of engagements. A liar. A liar. A cheat. And a gold-digger. But it had been easier that way…

'Forgive me if I sound sceptical, but Lydia Lawrence in a caring role isn't something I find very easy to imagine. In fact, I find it rather laughable.'

To say he was bitter was an understatement! But she had suffered, too. God! How she had suffered! And with a flush tinging the pale translucency of her skin, she bit back, 'Go ahead and laugh! But if you're going to fling insults at me you'll only find yourself looking for someone to babysit tomorrow—or cancelling your valuable schedule altogether! Because whatever you think about me, I shan't take your insults lying down.'

Surprisingly, she had managed to maintain some calmness, although it wasn't in her nature to lose her cool. And now she saw the lines of his beautiful mouth compress—because it was beautiful. She had always thought so. From the moment she had first seen him at that press launch thirteen years ago. But it was a cruel mouth, too, that hinted at his brooding sensuality and which, at times, could quirk into a heart-stopping smile that could melt any woman's heart. Now, though, it only betrayed that he was checking himself from making some flaying response.

'I take it you've been told about Liam's...problems?'

That he's difficult? Hadn't Heather warned her about that?

'Yes.'

'And you think you can handle them?' Doubt was graven on his strong face, doubt and cold, unremitting judgement that brought her chin up again in unconscious challenge.

'If you think I can't, then you'd better let me go now.'

He laughed, showing teeth that were strong and white. 'Oh, no. Your walking in here might have knocked me sideways, Lydia. But I'm interested. Interested to see what time has done to soften a hard-bitten little opportunist like you. Don't think you're getting away that easily this time.'

His words cleaved through her, producing a raw pain which she took every effort to conceal from him.

She was glad, therefore, when the maid came into the room—the same slim, dusky-skinned girl who had shown her in—and Lydia used this diversion to walk away from him, over to the doors leading to the verandah.

The day, she suspected, had lost little of its heat, and the scent-filled warmth of the Bermudian evening enveloped her with the sweet fragrances of oleander and a frangipani she could see growing near the house, tinged with the headier freshness of the sea.

'For what it's worth, Blaine,' she murmured with her back to him when the girl had gone, because she had to tell him. She *had* to. 'I never took that money.'

His footsteps on the pale wooden floor struck an ominous note against the sudden ''gleep-gleep'' of a whistling frog, close at hand in the luxuriant foliage that trailed over the verandah, then another, joining the eternal chorus of the night.

'Liar.' It was a softly breathed sound at her shoulder, as gentle as it was condemning. 'What would you have me believe? That you tore that cheque up and threw it back in my father's face? Told him your love for me was more important than any amount he could offer you to get the hell out of my life?'

'No.'

'No, of course you didn't.'

Because Henry Caldwell hadn't given her that opportunity when he had offered her that sum of money which was eyebrow-raising even to a highly paid model. Because, rich and powerful, wanting to spare his son from discovering the truth about her, he had paid that draft straight into her bank account, to show Blaine just how easily she could be bought off after that fateful interview when he'd told her she could never marry his son.

'Didn't you think he would show me the statement?'

As if she needed proof, Blaine's words only confirmed what she already knew. 'You didn't take a chance on the risky business of a cheque in the hand, did you, my dearest? You wanted more security than that! Tell me, Lydia, was I the only one? Or have there been others? Did it become a way of life? Seducing men and then tossing them aside for the highest bounty you could get?'

She swung round, turning her back on the night-shrouded verandah, facing her persecutor with her face marked by the pain of remembering.

'I had reasons for doing what I did!' It was pointless telling him that she had sent that money back, sent back every penny, because of course his father wouldn't have told him that. That would have given her credibility in his son's eyes, perhaps made him weaken towards her, and Henry Caldwell had been determined that she would have no involvement with his family. Not then. Not ever.

The reality of that still tore at her with lacerating claws, and through an anguish that tightened her lips with restrained emotion she heard the man say, 'What reasons, Lydia?'

He was waiting. So what could she tell him? The truth?

There had been countless times at first when she had wanted to explain to him. Make him realise that she had had no choice. Anything other than that he should so despise her! But she had been too afraid. Of his father. Of herself. Of how Blaine himself might have reacted. And then, of course, he had married Sharon...

'I was no good for you, Blaine. Let's just leave it like that, shall we?' she uttered, her agonies hidden behind a defensive barrier of calmness. 'Your father was right to protect you from me. And it didn't do you any harm,

did it?' Her gaze encompassed the tranquil elegance of
the spacious room.

Large cedar-framed doors and windows comple-
mented its pale floor and walls, which were respectively
graced by richly patterned rugs and original paintings of
bright Bermuda landscapes. Every little touch was taste-
ful, the furnishings very, very expensive, she concluded,
and, glancing back at Blaine, noticed that his expression
was one of hard contempt.

'Still the same old Lydia. You still think money's the
key to everlasting pleasure and fulfilment?'

Was that what he believed?

'No,' she uttered through a well of torment, realising
just how harsh his opinion of her was. And with her
eyes fixed on his, quietly she breathed, 'Believe it or
not, Blaine, I never did.'

For several moments his gaze locked fast with hers,
and something in the fathomless depths of his eyes tore
through her, producing a piercing ache way down inside.

She should have left, she tried advising herself hectically. When she had first realised who the boy's father
was! And, needing to break the treacherous spell that
held them, hastily she was enquiring, 'So where is
Liam?' She sent an almost desperate glance towards the
cedar door through which she had come earlier. 'When
can I meet him?'

'Tomorrow.' As though he were battling with some
inner demon, Blaine sounded breathless, his tone
clipped. 'I'm afraid he wouldn't wait up, though he was
asked to, though normally it's the devil's own work to
get him to go to bed. Such is my son's disinclination to
co-operate. I think you should know that he's both headstrong and rebellious…'

'That's encouraging!' Lydia pulled a face. 'Is that why you needed a nanny at such short notice? What happened? Did his last one walk out?'

The phone pealed on a marble-topped table and he looked at it with some impatience before it stopped, obviously answered in another part of the house.

'Something like that. And you might think it's something to be treated flippantly, but personally I don't think you'll be able to handle it, dearest. He's got a real grudge against authority and has had since…well, since his mother died.' There was a dark grief in him which Lydia recognised with harrowing realisation now; grief for the woman he had loved and lost so tragically, despite all his intimations of having been so wounded by her, Lydia. How could she have imagined anything else? 'He's got a mind of his own and will stop at nothing to get his own way…'

'Like his grandfather.'

Before she could stop it her pain was unravelling itself on a small skein of bitterness, and she saw that strong face tighten in chastening response.

'Before you start blaming him for your own scheming little actions, perhaps I ought to point out—if you aren't already aware—that my father died three months ago.'

And therefore she had no right even considering speaking ill of him. That was what he was saying. But of course she had known. News of the billionaire banker's death had been in all the papers. How could she not have known? Even now, guilt still assailed her for the lack of regret she had felt at the time.

'I'm sorry.' It was the right thing to say and it was all she *could* say. No other words could compensate for his double loss. But the harsh lines pain had drawn on his face, combined with that world-weary look about him, betrayed just how hard he must drive himself to rise above it, which only served to remind her of what a close-knit family they had been. Close, influential and impenetrable, which was why Henry Caldwell had refused to allow it to be touched—in any way at all—by the discredit he knew his son's fiancée would bring.

The maid returning with the refreshments interrupted Lydia's troubled thoughts. Silently she watched the young woman set down the silver tray with its two gleaming silver pots, the fine china cups and plate of luxurious, assorted biscuits, then heard her telling Blaine that he was wanted on the phone.

He strode out of the room, clearly not intending to discuss business or anything else in front of her, but the pretty little maid chatted to her as she poured their respective beverages and then retreated with a courteous discretion that could only have been expected of Blaine's household staff.

Only the best was good enough for the Caldwell family, she thought, picking up her cup and saucer and moving outside.

Here on the wide, covered curve of the verandah, the warm air and the whistling night creatures relaxed her a little. She strolled over to the iron rail, sipping her tea.

It was dark, but there was sufficient exterior light in places to see beyond what she presumed was lawn to the rocks the house was built above, and, way down, through the darker reaches of the garden, the illuminated water of what would naturally be a very private cove.

Yes, only the best for the Caldwells, she reiterated silently. Five generations of merchant bankers whose name went hand in hand with success, and whose heirs had been reared to expect perfection in all things, right down to Blaine and probably now his spoilt little son, Liam. Not that she was resentful about that. She had had a taste of success, and it had been her fame that Henry Caldwell had made full use of to discredit her, setting up that supposed infidelity to turn Blaine against her, shielding his family from the slur she would have put upon it, while she had lost everything. The man she loved. Her reputation. Her sanity almost.

She had stepped back inside and was finishing her tea by the time Blaine came back.

'I'm sorry about that. As you can see, business never stops at the top.' Even that dry comment didn't quite produce an accompanying smile. 'Unfortunately, I have things to do. But Tina will show you your room and tend to your supper and anything else you might require,' he said, massaging the back of his neck as though to relieve some inner tension. 'And Simon will already have taken your case upstairs.' Meaning the greying, middle-aged man who had driven her here from the airport, Lydia deduced, remembering he had followed her, with her luggage, into the luxurious hall. 'I'll see you in the morning.'

And that was that, she realised, relieved to be saying goodnight to Blaine before the maid who had brought the tea invited her to follow her upstairs.

The house was a showcase of understated opulence, from the curving staircase to the touches of marble, mahogany and cedar that enhanced the style and elegance of subtle, softer furnishings.

At the top of the stairs was a bead curtain which seemed to serve no apparent purpose, but Lydia's frown gave way to a subtle lift of brows as Tina showed her into the room where she was to sleep.

As one of the world's most highly paid models, she had been used to luxury, but the suite—because it was far more than just a room—was something else. Three rooms, comprising a sitting-room, a room with a huge double bed and a bathroom, graced by a round white marble bath, were at her disposal. In the bedroom, her case stood on a cross-legged little iron table ready for unpacking, and her flight bag had been placed beside it.

'I hope you'll be comfortable,' the girl commented as she prepared to leave, having ascertained that Lydia wasn't hungry, that she had had a late dinner on the plane. 'If you want anything, just ring,' she invited hospitably, and then, in her pleasant, Transatlantic lilt, 'You sure you don't need anything?'

Only to be out of here, Lydia thought with a sudden aching poignancy, but merely smiled, shaking her head.

'No, thanks, Tina. Everything's fine.'

The girl grimaced. 'I hope you still think so in the morning.'

'Come again?'

Tina laughed. 'If you're looking after Liam Caldwell—then rather you than me!'

'Surely he can't be that bad…?' Unable to contain the question, Lydia saw Tina shrug.

'No, he isn't, actually. I think he's just misunderstood. He's got problems, it's true, and they're actually made worse by the fact that his mom isn't around any more. And did she dote on that boy! But then he wouldn't have the problem if she hadn't—' She broke off, probably realising her indiscretion. 'Oh, well, I'll see you in the morning. Sleep well.'

Lydia grimaced as the door closed behind the maid. She doubted if she would sleep at all, let alone well! The last thing she would have knowingly done would have been to come to Blaine's house, subject herself to his disdain and justified contempt. Whatever had been between them was in the past and it had to be left that way. She had to forget it. Pretend it had never happened.

Neither did she want to have to explain to him why she had behaved as she had. With the harrowing fact of Sharon, like a wounding though merciful door slamming on all that she and Blaine had meant to each other, Lydia had hoped never to see him again—never to be reminded—and wouldn't have been if she hadn't taken this job. But she hadn't come here of her own accord, without knowing all the facts, because Heather had handled it all…

She glanced at her watch. Here in Bermuda it was just past ten o'clock, but it would be the early hours now in England.

For a few moments she hesitated by the phone on the cabinet beside the bed, her fingers tapping agitatedly on the pale vinyl.

It would serve her colleague right if she did ring and wake her up, Lydia decided bitterly. Heather needed to explain one or two things. Like why she had allowed her to come here, knowing who Liam's father was! Because she would have known. It wasn't Caring Days' policy to hire out nannies without full details of the parents or guardians engaging them.

Slender fingers closed over the phone without actually picking it up. What was Heather trying to do? Bring them together?

That her friend knew that she had once been engaged

to Blaine Caldwell was without question. It had made
nationwide news—world news—in the gossip pages.
Just as their break-up had, Lydia remembered with stab-
bing intensity. Every cheap newspaper and magazine
had made a meal of her apparent infidelity with top
newspaper baron Jeremy Tyndall. That was the price one
paid for being a super-model. Lack of privacy. Exposure.
Taking the brunt of everyone's criticism and condemnation.

Because jilting a man from one of Britain's richest
and most respected of families had made her a target for
the tabloid press and earned her the name of "Super-
Tramp" with some of its sensation-seeking journalists.
Or perhaps it was the parties that she had thrown herself
into with almost reckless abandon after her broken engagement, the high life she had used to submerge her
anger and her misery that had done nothing to endear
her to the public at large. But they hadn't known everything. Not even the man who had so cruelly tried to buy
her off, and then devastated her with his disclosure, had
known everything.

If he had… Shudders racked her and she abandoned
the phone, wrapping her arms around herself as she felt
the past like a whirling vortex, threatening to suck her
in. If anyone had known the whole truth, and the darker
secret she had carried with her, then she didn't know
whether she would have survived.

CHAPTER TWO

SHE awoke to the repetitive sound of the kiskadee.

Slipping out of bed, Lydia went to the window and pulled up the venetian blind.

Away to the east the sun was dazzling, and, half-blinded, she caught a glimpse of the bird as it shot out from beneath the ferny arms of one of the large date palms that fringed the sloping gardens, like a yellow dart, shrieking its name for all it was worth.

She would have turned away then, intent as she was on ringing Heather. A glimpse at the bedside clock as she had stepped out of bed had shown it was barely seven o'clock. Still early here, she realised, although back in England Heather would be halfway through her Monday morning by now.

Despite everything that had happened, though—meeting Blaine last night, taking his contempt, reliving the bitter memories of the past—for a few moments she couldn't move away from the window, her surroundings holding her in thrall.

The house was set amidst beautifully maintained grounds, as she knew from the drive through its shadowy bowers the previous night.

Now, though, the lush vegetation and semi-tropical shrubs that had yielded their strange chorus from behind soft, concealed lights, greeted the sun in a profusion of colours.

Red and white oleander, with flowers like huge peri-

winkles, grew close to the house, while a hedge of vary-
ing hibiscus with large, single flowers of rose, peach and
violet created a colourful pathway to a narrow stone jetty
and the cove.

She had never been to Bermuda before. Her career as
a top model had taken her to many fascinating and exotic
places, but somehow this lovely island had never been
included among them.

Her gaze lifted to the sea, sapphire streaked gold by
the sun. Its cobalt depths turned pale aquamarine where
it lapped gently against the small jetty, protected from
the full onslaught of the ocean by the huge harbour that
separated the stretch of land on which the house was
built from the most easterly reaches of the island.

No, you can't go out there. With an immense effort
of will she dragged herself away from the window. You
have to ring Heather. Ask her what she's playing at.
What was the code for the UK?

A very helpful operator connected her almost at once,
but the line was engaged. And engaged.

'Thanks, I'll try later,' she told the operator, when it
became clear that Heather was preoccupied with one of
her chatty friends. So what should she do now?

The great outdoors beckoned, and yet…

Losing the battle with temptation, she rummaged
through the case she had been too tired to unpack the
previous night and found one of the bikinis she had hastily stuffed in two days before.

It constituted little more than three scraps of white
linen trimmed with matching lace, and, pulling on a
white thigh-length tunic-top as a cover-up, she grabbed
one of the pale fluffy towels from the rail in the *en suite*

bathroom, and made her way rather stealthily along the landing.

Like someone who shouldn't have been there, she thought, and, with some unidentified emotion clutching at her heart, knew that for her own sake she shouldn't have been.

However, highly varnished doors remained closed on rooms still wrapped in sleep, and Lydia stifled a gasp as the bead curtain she had to pass through just before the stairs threatened to betray her with its useless jangling.

Surprisingly, the glass doors in the room where she had first encountered Blaine last night were unlocked, and quietly she slid them back and stepped outside.

The air was sweet, imbued with the perfume of a thousand flowers, and the thick warmth of the morning surprised her after the cool air-conditioning inside.

Two sets of wooden steps led down from the verandah—one onto the lawn, the other, which Lydia opted for, onto the path that skirted a terrace with a Grecian-style pool and brought her through the lush vegetation of the garden into the small cove.

A couple of boats bobbed alongside the narrow stone jetty, sleek white craft, with high-powered engines at the rear. The water lapped gently around them and a fish jumped, making a huge splash beneath the dark volcanic rocks immediately below the lawn at the back of the house.

The night creatures still whistled in the hibiscus hedge as she came down some stone steps onto the beckoning curve of pink sand.

Way off, across the glittering water, almost lost in a heat haze, she could see, with a hand shielding her eyes, the Causeway, which linked St George's Parish to the rest of the island. She had crossed it yesterday, coming from the airport, she remembered, where she had caught her first glimpse of the impressive hotel resort she could see now as she looked westward, a white spectacle of sloping terraced rooms that seemed to rise out of the sea itself.

And goodness! Could she do with a swim?

She had slept, but her dreams had been troubled by the shock of meeting Blaine. She needed the freshness of the ocean to revitalise her, give her the mental strength to face him again today, and, discarding her sandals and tunic, she ran towards it now as though to a saviour, wading through the translucent green shallows before plunging in.

The water was warm. Eighty-two degrees. Wasn't that what the airline's in-flight magazine had said? And it was. Incredibly warm and deep and buoyant, so that she emerged after a while feeling ready for anything, towelling her hair with one hand as she came up the beach towards the spot where she had discarded her cover-up.

A sound above her made her look up as she was about to retrieve it.

Blaine stood at the top of the stone steps, saying nothing, simply watching her.

He was wearing a short-sleeved white shirt and tie, with black flannel Bermuda shorts and knee-high matching socks, and from his elevated position, with the long façade of the sprawling white house behind him, he looked all that he was, lean and strong and powerful, and still as dynamic as he had ever been, more so for that hard-edged maturity he now possessed.

'I thought I was the only one up!' she called out,

disconcerted at having been caught semi-naked while he was clearly dressed for business.

'Did you?' His words were succinct, his tone flat. 'You'll have to do better than that if you want to catch me napping. This might be the right side of Paradise, but some of us do still have work to do.'

'Evidently.' What was he implying? That she had no right to a morning swim? 'No one told me I had to start at six o'clock.' She continued drying her hair.

'Did anyone suggest that you should?'

Well, no, he hadn't, she thought. So perhaps it's just me being over-sensitive.

He moved so that one foot was resting on the top step, one hand splayed across a very masculine knee.

'You're not quite the thing I envisaged for my son's nanny,' he remarked, his intimation clear above the distant drone of a small plane taking off from the airstrip over two miles away.

She imagined it, wings strewn with silver, climbing into an equally clear sky.

'I'm not a thing, Blaine,' she advised quietly, towelling the other side of her hair. 'And, as I told you last night, you'll soon have a replacement.' As soon as she could get through to that darned Heather!

With dark lashes concealing the turmoil in her eyes she didn't see the wry face he pulled, only heard his voice, dry with sarcasm, saying, 'Can you promise me she won't look like you?'

That grey gaze she met now was tugging insolently over her figure, and she brought her arm swiftly down, suddenly self-conscious at how much of her flesh was on view.

Her breasts had grown fuller with the years. But her

waist and hips still bore that model-leanness above long, well-shaped legs, and she knew it was that slender, almost fragile appearance about her that often made people unaware of how tall she was until they were standing next to her, although she carried her five feet nine inches with pride and an unconscious grace every bit as inherent as Blaine's.

'That innocent white lace doesn't quite go with the image of the lovely *femme fatale,* does it, darling?'

The frogs' and lizards' song had ceased now, silenced by the full strength of the sun, and Blaine's words dropped into the abyss, achieving what he had intended them to do—to effectively wound.

'If you're going to keep up this constant vendetta with me, Blaine…' tensely, Lydia slipped her feet into her sandals '…then it isn't going to work.' She couldn't bear it! Not for the shortest period could she begin to bear it.

His mouth twisted with something akin to contempt, although those eyes that continued to lay claim to her body burned with a fervency that held something more than anger, something that told her that despite everything—his hatred of her, the fact of his loving someone else, even his grief—amazingly he still desired her.

Something throbbed way down in her loins, and now the feelings which until last night she had thought sufficiently crushed by time rose again, like a long-trapped bird from a cage, along with her small, inaudible groan of despair: feelings that terrified her as they could never have done thirteen years ago.

Sick from the realisation of her own vulnerability, for a moment she thought she saw a bleakness in his face that she couldn't define, then decided that the sheer fear of herself was making her imagine things as he uttered with a clipped command, 'Get dressed, Lydia,' and turned and strode back to the house.

Dear God! She had to get away from here!

Quickly, Lydia retrieved her cover-up and, after pulling it over her head, tied the cotton belt around her waist and raked back her wet hair before following after Blaine. Heather was going to be told a few things if she *had* arranged this—

'Oh, Lydia!'

As she came up the steps onto the verandah, Tina's cheerful voice drew her attention to where the maid was standing, beside a small round table, laid for one, looking out towards the rocks.

'Blaine thought you'd appreciate your breakfast out here.'

That his staff were on first-name terms with him didn't surprise her half as much as that suggestion of his regard for her comfort, however small.

She would have liked to have changed first. Apart from which, after that little interview with Blaine, she didn't really feel like eating. But Tina seemed so happy to be catering for her that Lydia sat down and tried to do some justice to the orange juice, basket of blueberry muffins, croissants and pot of tea that was already on the table, causing her to realise that Blaine must also have informed his kitchen of her preferences. Maybe he had remembered her disinclination for cooked food in the morning, her love of sticky pastries. Remembered that, even as a model, at the height of her career, she could eat anything without putting on a pound. The thought that he might have considered her at all produced a dull ache in the pit of her stomach.

'Blaine never eats breakfast,' Tina supplied, coming

back to the table at one stage, the hard white glaze of the teapot she picked up accentuating the smooth, dark beauty of her skin. 'Sometimes I think that man exists on pure energy alone! He only takes coffee. Thick and black and strong! "I don't need anything," he says, "as long as I've got my cup of morning sunshine!" Or rather, he used to. Nowadays…' Her words tailed off on a little shrug.

Lydia lifted her gaze from the spiral of amber liquid refilling her cup. Yes, that sounded like Blaine, the young, happy Blaine she had known before. But that note of regret she had detected in the younger girl's voice only served to inform her that she wasn't alone in thinking that he had changed. He was hard now, hard as steel and twice as cold—cold and cynical—and she wondered if loving someone too much had done that to him, loving and then losing them as he had with Sharon.

What was left of her appetite deserting her, Lydia took a few more sips of her tea just to be polite, and excused herself. She felt deflated—almost depressed now—and told herself she had no right to feel that way. Whatever this family's problems, they didn't concern her, did they? she assured herself firmly. It was none of her business. She had to make that call!

Sweeping back through the lounge, keen to reach her room, as she came past one of the marble-topped tables, clumsily she kicked something over, heard it clatter onto the cool pale wood underneath.

With a small sound of concern, she was about to pick up whatever it was when a young, petulant voice behind her complained. 'Couldn't you look where you were going?'

Lydia swung round, meeting the unexpected hostility

on young features that were so much like Blaine's, from those grey eyes and rather hooked nose to that thick shock of dark hair, that for a moment she couldn't utter a word. He even seemed to possess the same haughty arrogance as Blaine. But he wasn't even looking at her.

In jeans and a dark T-shirt, a can of cola in his hand, he was scowling at something just past her shoulder.

She glanced behind her, shrugged, and, trying to keep her pique reined in, turned back to say, 'I guess I'm guilty of dashing around too fast.' This with an apologetic smile. 'You must be Liam. Hi. I'm Lydia.'

She held out her hand, which he totally ignored, instead enquiring rather rudely, 'What have you done with my stick?'

Lydia frowned. 'Your stick?'

She looked down and saw the thin, pale cane she had inadvertently kicked under the table, and not until she had picked it up and was handing it to him, had seen the way he kept looking straight ahead as he groped for it, did realisation dawn.

'Hi,' she uttered again, swallowing against the sudden contraction of her throat. 'Did your father tell you I was going to be your new nanny?'

She didn't know why she had said that when she didn't even intend staying. For something to say, she guessed, because this startling, unforeseen discovery had shaken her to her roots.

'I don't need a nanny.'

Liam's comment was swift and unexpected, and Lydia took a deep breath before trying again.

'It seems your father thinks you do. Who's going to look after you when he isn't here?'

The boy's lip curled upwards in a rather derisive fashion. 'I can look after myself.'

He swung away from her, stumbling headlong into the back of one of the long, low comfortable settees, and Lydia's response was to reach out and grab him before he could lose his balance.

'I don't think that's entirely true,' she said gently, having not yet recovered from the shock of Blaine's son being blind, although she could see some sense in a few things now. The bead curtain, a book she'd noticed in her room to do with helping the blind.

'Get off me!' He threw her hand aside. 'I don't need you! I don't need anyone!'

'Everybody needs someone at some time,' she continued in the same gentle tone, ignoring his rebuff.

'*He* doesn't.'

'He?' Lydia frowned down at Liam's sullen young face. 'Your father?' she pressed more quietly. And when he didn't answer, added, 'I'm sure he needs and loves you very much.'

'What do *you* know?' It was the accusing cry of a disillusioned adolescent, the way it ripped into Lydia shearing and profound. 'He doesn't want me! I just embarrass him!'

'That's not true!' She couldn't believe that of Blaine. Not the Blaine she had known. Concern lined her face. The boy had to be imagining it. 'How long have you been…unable to see?' She put it in the most sensitive way she could, only doing so because he had brought it up.

'What's it to you?' Again that same shunning tone.

'I'm interested, that's all.'

'Why don't you ask *him?*' His dark features were

glowering above the red and white aluminium of the can he was still holding, and then, with deprecating emphasis, 'You're his *girl*friend, aren't you?' he snarled.

'Liam!' Blaine's voice came with whip-cracking sternness across the elegant living room, startling Lydia as much as his son's description of her had. She could only surmise that the boy must have overheard something they had been saying earlier outside. 'You'll kindly do Miss Lawrence the courtesy of apologising to her.' Blaine's words were steel-edged, albeit that they were surprisingly soft.

Slamming the can down on the table, so that some of the dark liquid splashed onto the pale marble, the boy made a move towards the verandah.

'Liam!'

'It's all right, really, Blaine!'

As he swept past her, unconsciously Lydia's hand shot out to clasp his forearm. She felt the muscles bunch, that warm flesh pulse hard beneath her fingers, the startling contact shocking her into withdrawing them immediately even as he said, 'It's not all right!' He looked visibly shaken, as though her reckless touch had affected him as profoundly as it had affected her. 'It's downright inexcusable.' There was a controlled fury in the rigid muscles of his face, an implacable anger in the grey gaze directed at the boy.

'It always is!' Insubordinately, Liam was swinging away towards the sliding doors, and so fast and awkwardly that he fell against another table, sending what looked like a priceless glass vase that had been sitting in the centre flying. It struck the hard floor yet, miraculously, didn't break.

'Now pick it up!'

Liam seemed in two minds for a moment, but the steely command in Blaine's voice won over outright rebellion.

Horrified by such conflict between father and son, Lydia felt her heart twist as she watched the boy grope fruitlessly for the unfortunate vase. She took a step forward to help, but was stalled by the swift reflex action of hard fingers on her upper arm.

'No. He has to learn to do these things himself.'

But he's only a boy! She wanted to scream her thoughts aloud, but it was her eyes that said it, dark sapphire pools of condemnation and disbelief clashing with the stormy grey of Blaine's as Liam found the vase, groped unceremoniously for the table, where he dumped it down, before heading out of the door, striking the metal frame needlessly hard with his cane.

'Weren't you rather unnecessarily harsh?' Lydia reproached, feeling his touch still burning her arm even after he had released her.

'Harsh?' His tone was contradictory as he picked up the cola can and wiped the spilled drops from the pale marble, his long hands tanned against the folded white handkerchief he had taken from the pocket of his Bermudas. He dispensed with both can and handkerchief on Tina's tray as she was passing, looking rather uneasy at having walked in on Blaine's wrath. 'How else would you have me deal with a rude and disobedient twelve-year-old?' he challenged as Tina made her hasty exit towards the kitchen.

'Rude and—' Lydia broke off, totally flabbergasted. She had been able to feel Liam's frustrations. 'He's blind, for heaven's sake!'

Blaine's chest tightened as though she'd just hit him

in the solar plexus, his mouth taking on uncompromising lines.

'Yes, he's blind,' he affirmed heavily, as though facing a truth he didn't want to admit. 'And any unnecessary pandering to it on my part isn't going to equip him for an even harsher world out there!' Unwittingly Lydia's gaze lifted to the garden his jabbing finger had indicated. The tap of Liam's cane could still be heard over the stone steps leading down to the beach. Farther off, a gull shrieked its plaintive cry before it came into her vision, sleek, long-tailed and graceful as it dived, skimming the surface of the turquoise water, looking for fish. 'No son of mine is growing up to be a namby-pamby—and that includes Liam. If he's absolved from moods and rudeness now—given preferential treatment because of his disability—he'll expect it all his life. He's given the same amount of affection and discipline—no more, no less—that I would give to any normal child.'

'Are you saying he's abnormal?'

Impatience etched his features as he met her belligerent expression, his gaze moving briefly over her short, dishevelled hair and the tunic that clung to her damp bikini, showing off her long golden legs. 'Don't put words in my mouth, Lydia.'

'All right, then. But do you think your idea's fair, seeing he has so much more to battle with than your…' she refused to say "normal" '…average child?'

'My dear girl…' A hard condescension had replaced the anger in his voice, breaking through into derision, biting and cold. 'When did you ever know anything about being fair?'

His words sliced into ancient wounds that made her

want to cry out, *It wasn't my fault! I would never have left you! Not if I'd had a choice!*

Battling for composure, she decided to tell him instead that they weren't talking about her, but before she could he went on, 'Don't you think I don't know and understand what my son's needs are? He has special training. Hours of specialised instruction—'

'That isn't what I meant!' Liam needed love. A very deep and special understanding that his father was either too busy or too ill-equipped to give him. That wasn't difficult to see. But why was he like it? What was he doing? Running away from the truth—as she had run away from it over thirteen years ago?

'And I think your opinions would best be kept to yourself.' The chill in his voice was like ice across her raw emotions. 'I refuse to discuss Liam—'

'Why?' Her head shot up, cheeks splashed with heated colour. 'Because he embarrasses you?' As soon as the words escaped her she wished she could retract them, but it was too late.

A muscle twitched in the angry clench of his jaw, but there was a starkness to his face suddenly that made him look almost gaunt as he said in no more than a whisper, 'Is that what you think?'

No, that's what *he* thinks, silently Lydia responded, but she couldn't say that. She didn't want to alienate Blaine any further from his son than he already appeared to be.

'You weren't too keen on telling anyone that he was blind!'

Lines deepened across his forehead, around the corners of his narrowing eyes. 'You said you knew...'

'No, I didn't.' Now it was her turn to look puzzled.

'I…' She put a hand to her temple, trying to remember exactly what had been said. 'All I was told was that he was difficult…'

Her voice tailed off, her thoughts swimming in a whirlpool of confusion. And then through it she heard Blaine's words, relentless and hard.

'What's wrong, Lydia? Hasn't Bermuda turned out to be quite the picnic you'd imagined it would be?'

She didn't respond, her mouth firming as her head cleared enough for her to realise that she had been taken for a perfect fool.

Heather!

'What are you going to do now?' His question came cuttingly from behind her as she started purposefully towards the door. 'Simply disappear? Isn't that what you're best at when the going gets too complicated? When the immediate pay-off's better than the longer term commitment?'

Beneath the flattering 'V' neck of her tunic, her slender back stiffened. He would flay her verbally for as long as she cared to stay.

'Well?'

He was waiting for an answer. Anything that would give him the excuse he needed to carry on hurting her, vent himself of his frustrations, and not just for that mercenary betrayal he still believed she had been guilty of; not just because of the past.

She wasn't, however, going to give him that satisfaction, and she didn't even turn around before walking out of the room.

It was with a knowledgeable anger now that she pushed her way through the jangling curtain, taking out some of her own frustration on its heavily beaded strands.

In her room she went purposefully over to the phone and stabbed out her office number.

Heather answered almost immediately this time, her voice coming clear and confidently across three and a half thousand miles of ocean.

'What in heaven's name do you think you're playing at, Heather?' Lydia demanded without any preamble.

'Oh-oh! This sounds ominous.' Heather didn't need to ask who was speaking, her customary flippancy failing to amuse Lydia as it usually did.

'You knew, didn't you?' she breathed in positive accusation.

Another phone rang, far away, somewhere in the London office. Someone picked it up.

'Knew? Knew what?' Heather was playing the innocent. Stalling for time. Thinking of how best to talk her way out of another situation she'd taken it on herself to masterly manoeuvre, only this time Lydia wasn't prepared to be appeased.

'You knew it was Blaine Caldwell. You sent me out here deliberately—without giving me any idea of what I was getting myself into!'

There was a slight pause. Then, 'Yes. Guilty on all counts.'

Colour flushed Lydia's face. 'This isn't a joking matter! You should have told me the truth, Heather!'

The other woman made a wry sound. 'Would you have gone if I had?'

'You know darn well I wouldn't have!'

'Well, then...'

'There isn't any "well, then" about it! You didn't even tell me that Liam Caldwell was blind!'

Silence ensued for a few moments while Lydia considered the immense, dark body of water that separated them, separated *her* from the thirty-year-old blithe divorcee she dearly wanted to get her hands on.

'All right, so I wanted to get the two of you together. You and Blaine, I mean.'

'Why? What right did you have?' It was a poignant cry from the heart, and she didn't care if Heather did detect it, scarcely listening as her partner went on, undeterred.

'The right of someone who's concerned about a friend. A friend who's beautiful, detached and very, very lonely, and who won't even talk to a man who isn't either happily married, past it, or…well, you know. Lydia, I know how you feel about him. I've always known—in spite of what those abominable scandalmongers said about you.'

'How could you?' Lydia argued, recoiling from the reminder. 'You didn't even know me then.'

'I didn't have to,' Heather responded. 'I just know *you*. When that temp came last summer… You know, the one who'd just spent three months working in his office? You couldn't stop pumping her for information about him. Oh, I know we weren't supposed to realise it! But this old girl's shrewder than you seem to think. If someone mentions Caldwells—or you just see their name advertised on the side of a bus—you turn blue! And if that doesn't mean you've never got over him, I don't know what does!

'I know you didn't jilt him. Or, if you did, then I know you well enough to know you had a pretty good reason—and when his wife died—well, I couldn't get any sense out of you for about six weeks. You weren't with us half the time—only physically at any rate—and I just saw this as an opportunity to get you guys together—now that he's free. And I didn't tell you his boy was blind because I didn't want to say anything that might have put you off going.'

Put her off going! Lydia clutched the bodice of her tunic as though it could give her the physical support she suddenly felt sorely in need of. Heather didn't know. How could she? Regardless of that, though, she had had no right!

'You meddling, interfering, mindless…' She couldn't let the worst possible words escape her. She didn't want to be here, flinging insults at her friend. A friend she respected and cared about.

Down the line then, she heard Heather pressing, 'Go on—finish it. Mindless what? Mindless moron? I know I am, Lyddie, but that's part of my appeal.'

'You'll have to send someone else.'

'In heaven's name, why? Is it that bad?'

'Just do it, Heather!'

'I can't. Not at such short notice. It's asking the impossible. There's only Sarah, and she's off with tonsillitis. And Debbie, who won't fly. And I could have asked Pat, but the foolish girl's let her passport lapse. I can't do anything in under a week. Maybe two.'

Lydia's lashes came down against the weight of despair that was suddenly oozing through her. So she had to stay. Or just walk out, as Blaine had accused her of wanting to do.

'OK,' she said on a resigned note, and there was a

weary slump to her shoulders as she replaced the receiver and moved across to the window.

Someone had been in to make the bed while she had been downstairs, switching on the air-conditioning system and pulling down the blind to keep the room cool. So cool, in fact, that, in her still damp clothes, it made her shiver as she pulled the cord and peered out through the parted slats.

Liam was sitting at the end of the little jetty, feet dangling over the side, shoulders hunched as he stabbed at some unseen target in the crystal water with the inevitable distinctive white cane.

Lydia's heartbeat quickened as Blaine came into view, striding out from the screening hedge of hibiscus, heading straight down the jetty. He was wearing an immaculate white jacket now, over the black Bermudas, and carrying a document case which he tossed down into one of the moored boats before turning to issue some instruction to the greying-haired man who had also come into view.

Were they discussing her? she wondered, as Blaine sent a cursory glance up towards her room, making her draw swiftly back for fear of being seen. Or was he instructing his chauffeur to keep an eye on his son because the new nanny wasn't likely to be staying?

As the conversation broke up, Lydia's gaze followed Blaine's lithe figure to the end of the jetty, her eyes digesting every forgotten but now painfully familiar movement of his arresting physique.

He leaned over, said something to Liam, but the boy didn't respond, and something twisted inside Lydia as the man dropped to his haunches and placed an unmistakably caring arm around his son.

It was a glimpse of the old Blaine. One who once had shown that sort of tenderness towards her…

She clamped her clenched fist against her mouth, her teeth sinking hard into her tense knuckles as a devastating emotion swept over her.

Then, just as with her, she saw Liam fling his father's arm aside, saw the hard austerity in Blaine's features as, having got up, he swung grimly back along the jetty.

The growl of the boat seemed to reflect his mood as it turned out of the cove onto the open water.

Not quite the hassle of the London Underground, was her wry, distracted thought as her gaze rested on the straight, proud back of the man behind the wheel, cruising over the calm blue water. But envy was the last thing she was feeling.

And looking back at the boy who sat staring straight ahead, as though he could see the white roofs of the houses across the cove, the silver of the graceful gulls as they soared above the vivid ocean, something caught viciously at her heart.

She could just walk away. God! Why *couldn't* she just walk away? Because there was something more at stake here than just her feelings? What did Blaine matter to her? Or his son? They were another woman's responsibility. Not hers! He'd loved Sharon. Forgotten *her* years ago—as it had been only right that he should. So why couldn't she just abandon them in the way she felt she had been so effectively abandoned? Why did she feel as though she owed this family—owed Blaine—anything?

Because she did. And if she chose to stay—put her fears and her feelings on hold—because she knew now that they weren't dead, but lurking like dangerous spectres just beneath the surface—could she cope with that and his contempt? Because if she couldn't, the answer was simply to run away. Or tell him the truth.

CHAPTER THREE

POP music was playing loudly as Lydia stepped out onto the pool terrace, the sort of way-out beat to which even she was glad to consider herself too old to listen. Apart from that, at first there didn't seem to be anyone around, which made the music seem even more unnecessary and incongruous in such a peaceful setting. That was until she spotted the small bundle of clothes and cane lying beside the radio on one of the sun-loungers, and then Liam's head suddenly surfacing above the blue water explained.

Of course. The music was probably more than just recreational. He would need a landmark, some unseen pointer to guide him back to his clothes.

Her own simple sun-dress allowed the sun to caress her shoulders as she moved across the terrace. Reaching the radio, she stooped, turning the volume down for a second and then back up again.

It worked. Liam swam to the side and grabbed the tiled edge of the pool, his young face captious, his head slightly askance as he listened, trying to make out who was there.

'It's me, Liam,' Lydia called out brightly as he pulled himself up onto the side, and, before he could say anything, 'That's some pretty groovy music you're listening to!'

'Groovy?' His tone chafed at the rather old-fashioned word she had used as he stood up with the water running off him, tossing his wet hair out of his eyes. 'That's for old fogies—like grown-ups like listening to. Everyone always complains about the type of music I play.'

A flash of red caught her eye as a cardinal took off from one of the tall palms edging the pool and soared over the house, it's plumage dark as blood against the stark white of the roof. 'I seem to remember saying the same thing to my mother,' Lydia admitted truthfully after a moment, hoping her smile was evident in her voice.

That subtle attempt to show that she was on his side at least had him thinking.

'You aren't as old as he is, are you?' he stated, rather than asked, as he found his way easily to the source of the music, and even more effortlessly found the towel, thrown down beside the radio on the sun-bed.

He was tall for his age, like Blaine, she thought, as she watched him quickly drying himself, the lines and contours of that young body in striped boxer shorts promising the same muscular fitness as his father's in a few years.

'Him?' She cast a questioning glance his way. 'You mean your father?'

Liam didn't answer, and, stealing another look at him as he tossed the towel back down, Lydia detected the returning hostility in his face.

'About what you said earlier…' She saw him groping for his T-shirt, made a move to help him and thought better of it just before his fingers closed on the garment. 'I'm not his girlfriend.' Because that was the truth, wasn't it? 'I knew your father a long time ago. But that *was* a long time ago. He didn't even know I was coming.'

She hoped he believed her. For some reason it seemed

very important that Blaine's son should see her as a friend. And perhaps he had picked up on that sincerity in her voice, because suddenly he said, opening up again, 'He's always working, always going away.'

There was an injured note underlying the resentment in that young voice, and gently Lydia responded, 'He's a very busy man.'

Beneath the beat of a new number on the radio, she caught his cynical snort.

'He didn't used to be.' He was tugging on his T-shirt. 'Not that busy.'

She frowned, watching his dark head emerge through the hole in the navy blue fabric.

'Sometimes pressure of work can take us away from those we love,' she tried to explain carefully.

'It didn't used to. Not so much. Not when Mum was alive,' he startled her by saying as he searched around for his sandals with an impatient foot. 'It's just me…'

'Don't be silly,' Lydia advised, using her toe to subtly push the errant flip-flops that were lying near the sun-bed closer for him to find, then wished she had been more cautious in her attempts to reassure him when Liam's response suddenly turned aggressive again.

'What do you know?' he accused, thrusting his feet into the dark plastic, all set to fight her once more. 'I might have guessed you'd take his side!' And with that he snatched up his radio and, with his cane tapping the red herringbone tiles of the terrace, made a surprisingly swift departure back to the house.

When she went back upstairs she could hear the radio still playing, but more quietly now, in Liam's room, and, deciding it was best to leave him for a while, she went along to her own room to unpack.

Her clothes were badly creased from having been too long in the case, and she hung them carefully in the extensive wardrobe, folding underwear and casual tops in fragrantly lined drawers.

Afterwards, looking in on Liam, she found him reclining on his bed in a dry T-shirt and shorts, engrossed in something he was reading in Braille.

'Do you know your way around the grounds?' she asked casually.

The answer was a mere shrug.

'I'd love to see them. But I really need someone to show me around, Liam.'

'I've got to study this.' Resting on an elbow, he didn't even glance up. She could only presume it was something Blaine had instructed him to do.

'Are you staying in here for a little while?' After all, she was responsible for him, wasn't she?

'I'm not a baby.' It was a swift, petulant remark before he added sulkily, 'I'm not going anywhere.'

'Promise?'

'Yeah, yeah.'

Lydia shrugged, closing his door. She supposed she'd have to be content with that.

Outside, she took a few calming breaths, feeling the air like a sauna in her lungs, before taking a path through the foliage around the side of the house.

Blaine's Bermuda home, she could see now, was built on a narrow peninsula. A spit of land where one waterfront estate bordered another.

Above a hedge of thick vegetation, dwarfed by the occasional plantings of palms, she could see the outbuildings of another mansion, their white terraced roofs—which she now realised were a pleasing feature of Bermudian architecture—like icing on a wedding cake, reaching up to a powder-blue sky.

On the way from the airport the previous evening, Simon had said that Blaine seldom used the car when he was here. That it was mainly for the boy's benefit that he was employed and that Mr Caldwell preferred to conduct most of his off-shore business from the house, and she could understand why.

One path led down to the cove where she had swum earlier that morning, but on this side, through an avenue of citrus trees, the land fell away to rocks and a much larger beach, where the sparkling aquamarine ocean rushed, freely and undeterred, warmed by the coral-crushed sand.

She turned back along the grove. Overhead the green fruit of as yet unripened lemons bore testimony to the island's sub-tropical climate. The sweetness of oleander blossoms filled her nostrils. She saw them then, their rose-pink petals creating a profusion of colour against the pristine architecture of the house, the gentle hum of insects that surrounded it hinting at a false serenity that made her sigh. How could a place so lovely hold such turmoil within its walls?

The burr of a launch caught her attention, coming around the peninsula, its engine noise decreasing as it turned in the cove.

Blaine?

Tension gripped her insides. She hadn't expected him back so soon. Or perhaps she hadn't realised how long she had been out.

She couldn't see the cove from here, but she was certain it was him, and on impulse her reaction was to go deeper into the garden, submerge herself beneath the beckoning shelter of the citrus grove.

I must be mad staying here—for however short a time—if every time I see him I'm going to react like this, she thought eventually, squaring her slim shoulders and steeling herself to turn back along the path.

A movement startled her at the end of the avenue of trees, and her stomach muscles tightened as a less than friendly pair of eyes watched her progress along the grove.

'So you stayed?'

There was surprise beneath that frosty, perfectly English voice of Blaine's.

'I thought that was what you wanted,' she uttered when she was just a couple of metres away from him. He had discarded the white jacket she had seen him wearing earlier, the short-sleeved shirt and Bermudas exposing the hard tan of his sinewy limbs.

His gaze ran assiduously over the blue sun-dress that showed off her smooth shoulders and the long length of her legs, and now she could see that his face was etched with angry lines and that his eyes were furious.

'In that case what the hell do you think you're playing at, dismissing my chauffeur and letting Liam wander off by himself? He was walking dangerously close to the rocks when I came in just now, and if I hadn't come back when I had, heaven knows what might have happened to him! If you've chosen to stay then your place is with him—not off in search of some amusement of your own!'

So Liam had defied her. Broken his promise.

'When I left him he was safe enough,' she informed him, deciding not to betray the child entirely, tell Blaine that his son had promised her he'd stay in his room. 'And Simon asked *me* if we'd be needing him this morning because he wanted to get the car looked at,' she enlarged, with colour spreading high across her cheekbones. 'It wasn't my idea!'

He made a sceptical sound through his nostrils. 'Do you call it safe, leaving a blind child where anyone with half a brain—where even he—knows it's out of bounds for him to be on his own?'

But he had gone there anyway.

'Perhaps if you gave him more of your time—didn't bully him quite so much—he wouldn't be so ready to disobey you!' she couldn't help remarking, refusing to shoulder all the blame when she was, after all, the only innocent party in all this.

'Is that what you think I do? Bully him?' The shadows from the lemon tree under which they were standing seemed to harshen the dark contours of his face. 'Maybe that's your interpretation of it, but personally I just want to make life easier for him, that's all!'

From the tension that held his features rigid it was evident he had the boy's interests at heart, while Liam wasn't making it at all easy for him.

Lydia tore her gaze away from him, her heart swelling with sympathy for him in his role as a lone parent as she started walking back towards the house.

'He was always a wilful child, but he's been impossible—I suppose understandably,' he appended, falling into step beside her, 'ever since he lost his sight.'

Lydia caught that ragged note in his voice, suddenly aware that he was opening up to her.

'How did it happen?' she prompted, with a degree of circumspection now.

There was a long pause, and a guarded sideways glance at him showed pain etched, soul-deep, in those arrogantly proud features.

'I would have thought you'd know.' His voice was cold, dispassionate. 'He cycled out in front of Sharon's car the day she hit that tree.'

Lydia stopped, standing stock-still as he was. Her face was pinched with shock. 'You mean...it was because of Liam...' She brought herself up sharply.

'It could have been worse,' he stated flatly. 'I could have lost them both.' But beneath that prosaic tone was a hardness that only came from some devastating hurt, and she wondered just how deeply he had loved the petite redheaded socialite, and then, with startling clarity now, wondered how much he blamed Liam for her death.

'It must be tough for him—not just losing his sight, but losing his mother like that,' she expressed when he just stood looking out across the grass that hemmed the front drive and the main gates to the road that ran back along the peninsula to the main stretch of the island. 'Tina—' She stopped short. It was hardly prudent, repeating what one of the maids had told her.

The light breeze ruffled his thick hair as he gave her his undivided attention now. 'Yes, what did Tina say?'

Lydia took a stalling breath. She guessed it didn't matter. 'That Sharon doted on him.'

'Tina said that?' Some dark and private emotion seemed to stretch the skin taut across his cheekbones. 'I'm sure everyone would have said the same thing,' he remarked, and then, with his expression shuttered, 'She was the perfect wife and mother.'

And you? Did you dote on her? her heart clamoured,

wrung by the austerity in his voice which she could only guess sprang from the depths of his feelings for his late wife. But she didn't say it aloud. She had no right to wonder. Or to feel the pierce of this crucifying anguish. No right at all!

'He was always a good kid—albeit rebellious,' he was saying absently, as though to himself, as though she weren't really there. 'For all that wild streak he always managed to get down to whatever needed doing—taking top marks in most subjects at school. Now I have to push him every step of the way.'

With his features set in a grim cast, he looked so much like the petulant boy who was causing him so much anxiety that it was suddenly easy, as they were walking on again, to visualise him as the child he must have been—brooding and clever—like Liam—almost uncontrollably headstrong—and with a father who would shape and direct his life with whatever it took.

'Perhaps you're pushing him too hard,' she ventured to suggest quietly, feeling like the lamb challenging the indomitable strength of the lion, especially when he sliced a withering glance her way.

'You just concentrate on your job—which is keeping him occupied and making sure he doesn't fall and break his neck while I'm not around—and leave the question of his upbringing to me.'

'And everything will turn out fine?' His condescending tone had rankled, putting a sharp edge to her response. 'I'm not eighteen any more, Blaine. I do have some experience of the world.'

They had come around to the side of the house, but he stopped dead now in front of her. 'I'll bet you have!' he said.

His obvious taunt cut through her, but she refused to give in to any childish retaliation. It was something she had learned, this control; learned it and cultivated it so that it hung like a dark cloud over her emotions. 'I thought we were talking about Liam? His needs. His difficulties.' Rather haughtily she pushed past him. 'I was just trying to offer you help, that's all.'

'You?' He almost scoffed at the possibility as he swung on his heel to follow her. 'What do you know about parenthood? You've never even had a bloody child!'

Something more than his anger halted her footsteps along the stone path, blanching her cheeks, making her fine features stand out against the chic darkness of her hair.

'Well, have you?' he demanded, his imperious tone alone forcing her to look at him. 'Have you ever been...*married*, Lydia?'

Those grey eyes searched hers, unpitying yet darkly unfathomable. She felt a lump in her throat, and had to force herself not to swallow. Way off a jet-ski hummed across her consciousness, an escalation of sound that throbbed through her senses until she could see the craft sweeping round in a wide arc just level with their peninsula, before it turned, full-circle, and sped off again across the bay.

'No, to both your questions,' she answered calmly at length, disguising the underlying turbulence left in their wake.

'Well, then...' He exhaled heavily, and she wondered if it was because he thought his point had hit home. 'I'd deem it a courtesy if you didn't interfere with the way I handle my own son—unless, of course, you have some special qualification for dealing with a disability like Liam's?'

His tone was mildly derisive, causing her mouth to compress, her breasts to rise and fall sharply at his audacity.

'None,' she said flatly, and took some warped pleasure then from being able to tag on, 'Except that my grandfather was blind.'

Only the breeze stirring the pink flowers of the oleander bushes bordering the estate filled the pregnant silence that followed.

Eventually, on a rather self-deprecatory note, he said, 'Is that something else I'd forgotten?'

She shrugged. 'Maybe I never mentioned it.'

She thought he caught his breath. 'Maybe you didn't. And I thought I knew everything about you.'

Did he?

She looked at him quickly, her pulses suddenly drumming.

'Evidently not,' he accepted. There was no distinct emotion behind the wry face he pulled. 'I just remember you as talkative. Talkative, and hungry for every scrap of knowledge and experience you thought it my responsibility to share with you.'

Oh, Blaine, don't...

She turned her head so that he wouldn't see the way her lashes lay across her eyes.

'Was I?' she murmured, not wanting to remember. It hurt to talk like this about the past with him, but she couldn't stop the memories from flooding back, no matter how hard she tried.

It had been a glorious summer, a respite for a lonely eighteen-year-old, an only child, whose father had deserted even before she was born, and whose mother had died from a swift and unexpected illness only the year before.

Being the daughter of an infamous actress hadn't been easy, especially when her mother had pushed her into the limelight at every opportunity. She remembered how she had wanted a more academic occupation for herself, remembered her dream—with her love of books and literature—of becoming a librarian, but her mother had considered that stuffy and too run-of-the-mill for her only daughter, insisting on, and financing, a modelling career.

With the looks she had inherited from her mother and her photogenic bone-structure, Lydia had been nevertheless amazed when her career had become almost an instant success, her face commanding a fortune, her figure sought after by the top fashion designers of the world.

And then she had met Blaine, and all that had mattered had been a future with the man she had fallen instantly in love with, a future away from the superficial glare of stardom. Their future, which overnight had turned from a sunny horizon to a blinding grey ocean of nothingness.

'I didn't realise... About your grandfather.' Blaine's statement dropped like a line into the sea of melancholy she had been lost in, hauling her gently back.

She shot a glance his way. Was that a genuine apology in his eyes?

'It was only in his last couple of years,' she said, shrugging it off, reflecting for a moment on the benign, white-haired gentleman who had shared a home with her when her mother was away filming—as she so often had been—and who had died when Lydia was fourteen. 'And he managed to cope very well.' She could see though that she had taken the wind out of those powerful sails and she couldn't help feeling a little smug.

'You're full of surprises, aren't you, Lydia?' he commented, clearly resenting the fact that she had got the better of him. 'But Liam isn't coping, as you put it. He's fighting his blindness just as stubbornly as he's always fought everything else. It's been over eighteen months now, and he's no closer to accepting it than he was at the beginning.'

Neither are you, she thought, seeing the bitterness in those arresting masculine features. And until you do, neither can he.

'I'm sorry,' she uttered, and, feeling for him, couldn't help adding, 'For both your sakes,' and knew she shouldn't really have been surprised when her commiserations were met only with what sounded remarkably like a snarl.

'Forget it,' he drawled succinctly. 'If that's sympathy you're offering, I don't need it, especially from Lydia Lawrence!'

'You weren't getting it, Blaine.' Hurt by his cutting snipe, she tried to sound unaffected, although she could understand his resentment. If she had been betrayed as he believed he had been all those years ago, she would probably have felt the same way. Worse, even, because at least he *had* married—and unimaginably quickly afterwards—and it was only the torturous reminder of that that stopped her from confessing everything, blurting out the truth.

'So…' They had reached the path running alongside the house, afforded some shade by some tall palms and the brilliant flame of two flowering poinciana trees.

'So?' she queried, lifting wary eyes to his.

'So let's talk about you.'

Her instincts shot into danger mode as he stopped on the path in front of her. Out of the corner of her eye, on the wall of the house, she saw the blue and green flash of a lizard as it darted for cover behind a purple bougainvillaea, and wished she could do the same.

'What did you do after you walked so unceremoniously out of my life? Or should I say after you dumped me like a piece of baggage that was superfluous to your requirements? Apart from date every available thing in trousers in London—and in just about every other capital it was considered fashionable to be seen in. What did you do after several months of earning yourself a somewhat dubious reputation, before you suddenly and effectively dropped out of sight?'

She hadn't thought it was possible for the scars she had thought were fading ever to open again. But now his words, with their reminder of that time, seemed to rub like glass-paper over their suddenly raw lesions, causing her to suck in her breath against the pain. Her voice, though, was surprisingly composed as she said in guarded response, 'Were you following my life so closely, Blaine?'

His eyebrows lifted at the question she had so carefully lobbed back at him. He was measuring its implication.

'I could hardly help it,' he commented drily. 'Any more than could the rest of the British public! Every time I picked up a newspaper your face was in it. Even the more up-market ones found space to print the latest update on Lydia Lawrence's love life!'

Her lashes came down, shielding her eyes and the dark

emotion they contained as she uttered, 'And of course you believed every word.'

He laughed, a low, cynical sound on the scented air. 'You forget,' he said softly, 'that I had first-hand experience of Britain's most infamous model. We made quite a splash ourselves when you jilted me for your short-lived fling with Tyndall. Or have there been so many since that you really don't remember?'

There was a cold hostility in those hard, keen eyes that chilled her to the bone. But all she said quietly was, 'Is that what you think, Blaine?'

Something about her composure seemed to annoy him. The lines of his jaw harshened as he dragged in a breath, uttered in an intimidating whisper, 'Does it really matter to you one way or the other what I think?'

Yes! For a moment she wanted to scream out again that there were reasons for the way she had behaved, that making him despise her was an easier option than watching him digest the truth.

But she hesitated too long and, with a heart-severing presumption, he said, 'I thought not. So tell me what you've been doing all these years. What spurred you into taking on a thing like Caring Days? Its cloak of respectability?'

It was a hook to snare her, but she refused to rise to his bait.

'Perhaps,' she breathed, humouring him. 'Who's interested in the day-to-day existence of a nanny? I needed a new career, and childcare was something I'd been doing—that I stumbled into after I gave up modelling.'

'And why did you? Relinquish that glorious career? I wouldn't have thought you could have lived without the limelight—without all the attention. So why give it up?'

Because it made me ill! Driving myself so hard to try and forget you! She put a stay on the chaotic response she would dearly have loved to fling back at him. He couldn't know, though, how she had hated the job she had taken on only to satisfy her mother. How she had hated the limelight of which he had so derisively spoken.

'Too much high living isn't good for anyone,' she murmured with a little shrug. Wasn't that what he expected her to say? 'I couldn't stand the pace.'

His mouth twitched cynically. 'And then?'

Then Gary had nursed her through her nervous breakdown and, at the end of it, persuaded her to take a job abroad, helping his cousin and her husband with their little girl.

'I took a job as a nanny for a friend of mine—found that I liked it. They were moving to South Africa and so I went with them. I looked after Lisa for several years while her parents worked, until she outgrew needing me. During that time I managed to study, get myself a qualification in business management, and went back to England after that.'

'That's when you opened up the agency?'

'No,' she said. It hadn't been quite that easy. 'For a time I was registered with one of the more established agencies in London.' It hadn't worked, though. Despite managing to keep a low profile with the press, her name and her face had been too famous for anyone to forget. Some households had been reluctant to take her on, while others had presented problems with the male members of the house, who'd imagined that her innocently acquired notoriety meant she'd be easy game. 'I met my colleague, Heather, through a friend of mine. She was administrator in a nursing home where his father was resident—'

'His?' He was looking at her obliquely, those grey eyes interrogative.

Lydia's shoulder lifted again beneath the fine blue strap of her dress. 'Gary. A photographer friend of mine.' In fact that was all Gary Marshall had ever been to her—a friend, albeit a very dear one. But she didn't consider it relevant to tell Blaine that. 'Anyway, Heather had all the right qualifications—administratively and in a caring capacity. We became friends, and started Caring Days four years ago.'

'And working behind the scenes is easier.' He couldn't keep the derision out of his voice, nor had he intended to.

'It's different,' she expanded, without giving him the satisfaction of a retaliation.

'That is until somewhere more exotic crops up and the lure is too great to resist.'

Lydia bit her top lip, but finally her rising resentment at the way he was treating her goaded her into snapping, 'That's right! Blow the responsibility. The location more than makes up for looking after someone else's spoiled brat!' Wasn't that what he wanted to hear? 'If you think that, then you don't know me, Blaine. You've never known me!'

'Haven't I?' Emotion shook that deep voice, and beneath his obvious anger she recognised an intensity of pain that rocked her. 'Because you never gave me the chance! Two months! That was all you gave me. I wanted you to be my wife! And I thought that was what you wanted too! You managed to convince me of it. And, God! We were close enough…!'

Her eyes closing tightly, she turned her head away. She didn't want to remember.

'All right. Dispute it now!' he rasped. 'But you know you managed to convince yourself you were in love with me. Either that—or it was a pretty damn near award-winning act! So why didn't you keep it up, Lydia? Why didn't you go ahead and let me marry you? Surely I would have been worth more to you in alimony—'

'Don't!' She would have swept away from him, but his hard body barred her escape route. He took a step nearer, and she flinched as his hand lifted suddenly to the perfect curve of her cheek, causing her to shrink back against the warm wall of the house.

'You're even lovelier now than you were then.' He made it sound like an accusation, though those cool fingers were moving with surprising gentleness along her cheek.

'Blaine, please…'

She couldn't tell him why she pulled away, why the shivering awareness of his touch stirred an ache so sweetly acute that it would have been easy to forget that that painful scenario with his father had never existed. That she wasn't…

No!

'We can't take up from where we left off, Blaine.'

She stood away from him on the path, emotion trembling through her slim body just as the breeze trembled through the leaves of the bougainvillaea climbing the house.

'Were you imagining I would want to?' He had gained control of himself now, all feeling contained behind that hard self-poise. 'Oh, no, Lydia. After all the grief you've caused to me and my family, I'm totally immune to your type of charms. Lovely you might be, but this is one man's skin you're never going to get under again!'

He turned and strode away then, broad shoulders held rigid as a shield against her.

Watching him, Lydia couldn't restrain the small sob that left her lips.

He despised her, and it was only natural that he should, she accepted bitterly. But what had he meant by the grief she had caused to him and his family? All right, she could have believed she might have hurt him thirteen years ago if he hadn't replaced her with his lovely Sharon—and so painfully quickly. But why was he accusing her of causing distress to his family?

Memories of the Blaine she had known—of the laughter and the tenderness—surfaced to stab her like a knife in the chest, so that she gave a small gasp, finding it difficult to breathe.

He hated her so much, he probably just wanted to hurt her, she thought, in any way he could, and, painful though the realisation was, she knew now that that was the least of her worries. The biggest problem, she realised, as she started after him around the path beneath the verandah, was that her feelings for him hadn't waned with the years. Impossible though it was, she was in danger of being affected by him just as powerfully as she had ever been, so that she found herself praying, as a wave of nauseous fear hit her with breath-catching force, that it wouldn't be long before Heather relieved her with her replacement.

CHAPTER FOUR

LIAM was sitting at the table against the far wall of his room when Lydia tapped lightly on his open door.

'You didn't tell him,' he said broodily as she came into the room with a view to asking him if he wanted something to drink.

She knew he was referring to Blaine.

'Tell him what?' she queried, pretending not to know.

'That you told me not to go off on my own.' He had his back to her, having been working at his computer, but he half turned now, gazing sightlessly across the space that separated them. 'Why didn't you?' He sounded surprised and puzzled that she hadn't.

Lydia moved over to him, her hand coming to rest on the back of his chair.

'Don't you think things are bad enough between you and your father without trying to make them any worse?' she put to him tentatively. She had shared lunch with them both earlier, and even then the atmosphere between Blaine and his son could have been cut with a knife.

Liam turned away, his young face darkening, and the next minute pencils and other small objects were scattering over the table from a desk-tidy he had knocked over.

'What are you looking for?' Lydia enquired, as his fingers fumbled over the stack of audio cassettes on one side of the table.

'My favourite tapes. I keep them on the left—separate

63

from the others. Tina's been in my room and mixed them all up!' An angry swipe of his right arm sent them clattering across the hard surface. 'I *told* her not to mix them up!' His left hand lay tense and claw-like on the table. It was a long, well-tapered hand, like Blaine's. 'Now I have to go through them all again!'

Lydia's heart contracted at his frustration, emotion spurring her to lay a compassionate hand over his.

Even as she did so she wished she could have stopped herself, but the rebuff she was expecting, surprisingly, didn't come. Instead, those young fingers caught and closed tightly for a moment under hers.

'I'll tell you what,' she said brightly, casually removing her hand before he could regret and rebel at the affection he so sorely needed. 'Tina has to come in to clean. But I can show you a way to stop your tapes getting mixed up. Have you got any elastic bands?'

Liam's black brows knitted above the young beak of his nose. 'There was one here...' He was groping over the sorry scattered contents of the table.

'Thanks.' Lydia smiled as he held up the little brown rubber loop. She took it from him. 'But we'll need more than that.'

The boy's frown deepened. 'In Dad's study,' he said. 'He used to keep lots in his desk.'

'Right.' She was almost glad Liam couldn't see the colour she could feel creeping into her cheeks.

He had, however, detected that hesitancy she hadn't been able to keep out of her voice, and that quickness of her breathing, she realised, when he enquired, 'Why are you nervous of him? I didn't think you were afraid of him.'

'I'm not afraid of him, Liam,' she said, putting him

straight, and swept out of the room before he could ask her what exactly she was afraid of, leaving the bead curtain jangling agitatedly behind her as she hurried downstairs.

The study was a large, cedar-panelled room at the front of the house, with wall-to-ceiling bookcases and classic furniture. A comfortable office where Blaine sat, with his back to the window, scribbling something as he bent over the large mahogany desk.

The high bright sun filtering in through half-closed blinds sent streaks of dark fire through his hair, and Lydia had to swallow, keep her sudden emotion in check, trying to sound as dispassionate as she could as she made her request.

'Rubber bands?' His mouth was twitching as he sat back against the padded leather of his chair, pulled open a drawer and after a few moments produced a small box. 'What are you going to do?' There was curious amusement in his eyes. 'Make a banjo? Or something more intriguing, like a catapult?'

'Something you should have done long ago,' she said crisply, snatching the box he was handing to her and, without any further explanation, made her speedy return to Liam's room.

'There...now it won't matter where your tapes are,' she told the boy some time later, after she had placed the rubber bands over the cases of various cassettes. 'Here...' She lifted one young hand to demonstrate to Liam how he could instantly recognise his favourite albums just by touch. 'Oasis and Blur have one band. Oasis' goes lengthwise; Blur's goes widthwise across the case—you have to remember that. Your rap music has two, and these classical albums...' she guided his fingers to the two albums of piano music she had been pleased to discover he liked '…these have three. Now, if they ever get mixed up again,' she said with a smile in her voice, 'you'll only have one person to blame.'

'Ingenious.'

Lydia swung round on hearing the deep, masculine drawl from the doorway, while Liam acknowledged his father's presence with only the barest movement of his head.

'Do you have any other tricks like that up your sleeve?' Blaine asked softly, coming into the room.

'Plenty,' she uttered shakily, because he had stopped just an arm's length away from them. 'And they're not ingenious. Just common sense,' she added on a little chastening note. 'Just that—and the little bit of time it takes to care.'

She saw him visibly tense beneath the pristine elegance of his clothes.

'Liam.' He ignored Lydia, glancing down at his son. 'Tina tells me tea is nearly ready, and that she's made one of her special cakes for you, so why don't you pop downstairs and find out what it is?'

So that you can be alone with me? To tear me off a strip for intimating that you don't care enough about him? Lydia thought, her throat going dry even as she heard Liam's protest.

'But Lydia was showing me things nobody else has taken the trouble to show me.' Surprisingly, it was a compliment. Rather unintended, she felt, but a compliment nevertheless.

'I'm sure she'll be happy to…surprise us all with her handy hints and practicalities.' There was something other than just mockery behind those carefully chosen words, Lydia detected, but couldn't decide what it was as Liam complied with his father's wishes and left.

Now get it over with, she thought as they stood facing each other in silence, ears tuned to the tap-tap of wood against wood as the boy made his way along the landing, to the jangle of beads that warned in advance of the imminent stairs.

'You might be good for him,' amazingly he told her then, as he strode past her and picked up one of the cleverly marked cassettes. 'God knows, he needs some-one!'

Lydia caught the inflexion in his voice and leaned back against the table, for some reason needing the support it offered her.

'Someone?' She glanced across at his taut, dark profile. 'What about you?'

He tossed the cassette down, staring at the cover photo of four intense young men gazing broodingly up at him.

'I'm too close.'

Too close? To close to what? she wanted to ask. The accident? The reminder—every time he looked at Liam—of his lovely Sharon? Of what his son's moment of innocent misjudgement had done to her? To them all?

'He needs someone who's detached from all this,' he said, with a jerk of his head towards the table and the Braille-writing machine, the loudly ticking clock that Liam used to help guide him across the room, the carefully sorted cassettes. 'Someone who won't run out every time he throws a tantrum.'

As his previous carers had? He didn't say it, but she knew that that was what he meant.

Those handsome features that so often in the past had been filled with sensual teasing for her were now darkly intent as he fingered one of his son's Braille books, and a lump caught in Lydia's throat.

He was still formidably handsome.

Unconsciously, her gaze ran over the hard angles of his face to the corded strength of his throat, visible now in the 'V' of his open shirt. His waist was still slim, his abdomen tight and flat. He could still hold a candle to a man half his age, she thought as she considered the latent strength in those bare forearms, thickly furred with dark hair that ran down the backs of his wrists to those long, tanned hands. That was one of the first things she had noticed and loved about him—his hands...

It was like tearing a magnet from a steel wall, trying to tug her gaze away from them.

'Blaine...' Her voice was no more than a trembling whisper. 'I don't know if I can stay.'

She didn't know because she wasn't sure if she could cope with the knowledge of how much he despised her; she couldn't cope—heaven help her!—with the knowledge of her own unthinkable attraction to him...

'You'd still leave?' His mouth was contorted with disbelief, and his tone was all condemnation now. 'In spite of the state he's in? Even with all the experience you've obviously had in dealing with a visually impaired person, you'd throw it all aside for...for what? Something less troublesome?'

Lydia swallowed and looked down at her Indian sandals, at the fine gold chain that made a 'V' across the centre of each before disappearing between her slender toes.

Outside, beyond the open window, a cardinal shrieked, leaves rustling as it took off with an agitated flapping of wings. Then all was restored to calm, save for the gentle wash of the waves on the coral beach beyond the citrus grove, soft and rhythmic and eternal.

'He won't be any trouble,' she said flatly, her back straight, her shoulders square as she walked determinedly away.

Blaine was out for the rest of the afternoon, and the following morning he flew off to New York, where he remained for the next three days.

During that time Lydia was able to relax more, at least where her emotions were concerned.

Coping with Liam, however, was a full-time job, and one which, surprisingly, she found herself enjoying. The boy needed a friend, a confidant, someone to talk to and laugh with. And although at first he did very little laughing, and confided in her even less, Lydia was very much aware of how rejected he felt by his father, and how important it was simply to be there if he needed to talk to someone. As Gary had been there for her years before, without even needing to know why, she remembered with a mixture of gratitude and sudden, aching emotion. When she had been at her lowest ebb...

This wasn't the place, though, to dwell on unhappy times, she thought that morning as she finished her breakfast, presided over by Tina, in the usual place on the verandah. Liam had already finished his and excused himself a little while earlier.

Content, therefore, to bask in the shade, with the frangipani tree exuding its fragrance from its creamy flowers by the path just below the verandah, Lydia had happily agreed to let him go.

She had to hand it to Blaine, though, she thought, because, difficult though Liam was, he did sometimes surprise her with the odd courtesy, obviously instilled in him by his father. Like pulling out her chair in one café they had visited—glad of its air-conditioned interior after the midday heat outside. Then he had groped his way around the table to his own seat, looking so much like Blaine that her breath had caught in her lungs.

She heard the quick tap-tap of the cane now on the pale wood of the living room floor before Liam stepped out, looking flushed and agitated.

'Dad's back,' he said, unaware of how her heart suddenly lurched on hearing the news. 'He just came in. Didn't you hear him?' That sullen expression, which had been absent for the past three days, was back.

'No, I didn't,' Lydia admitted. She had heard Simon drive out earlier, but the whine of a lawnmower being used by a groundsman—still cutting the grass on the other side of the house—must have drowned the sound of the car coming in again, she realised, robbing her of the chance to make a ridiculous escape to her room.

'Anyway, the good news is that my gran's been on a cruise and she's docking here today,' Liam went on to inform her. 'Dad just told me.'

Lydia saw a glimmer of pleasure light his young face before he negotiated the steps down to the garden, while she sat, with her features looking suddenly pinched, feeling her muscles tightening painfully in her stomach.

As far as Judith Caldwell was concerned, Lydia was just a gold-digger, bought off by Henry Caldwell not to marry the man she had professed to love. It was bad enough coming here and facing the agony of seeing Blaine again, without the added complication of his mother.

She wanted to flee, but there was nowhere to run, and

unsteadily she rose from her chair just as Blaine stepped out onto the verandah.

'Good morning.' He was all impeccable formality, from the dark business suit he must have been aching to get out of to the cool urbanity of his tone.

'Good morning.' Lydia was glad she could hide behind her sunglasses as stiffly she returned his greeting, then followed his gaze to the lonely figure of Liam, feeling his way past the unseen vibrant colour of the hibiscus hedges.

'Might it be too presumptuous of me to enquire if in fact I was missed?'

A degree of warmth behind Blaine's quip prompted her to turn and smile at him now.

'No, we've been far too busy,' she assured him lightly.

'Oh?' He was looking at her askance, with genuine interest in the smouldering grey gaze that touched briefly on her white cotton sun-top and yellow shorts, and so she told him.

'Liam took me on a guided tour of St George's.' Actually, it had been Simon who'd taken them to the island's old capital. But Liam had given her an insight into the picture-book town that had looked more like a film-set, with its pastel-coloured buildings, its old stocks and pillory on the square and residents who dressed up in seventeenth-century English costume for the benefit of tourists. He had shown her the replica of the *Deliverance*, the dubious-looking vessel that had taken Bermuda's first castaways to Virginia—their originally intended destination—in 1610. 'We also took a trip on a glass-bottom boat out to one of the old wrecks.' The reef around Bermuda, she had discovered, had claimed countless ships over the centuries. 'And Liam fed the fish.'

'The fish?' Now all urbanity was gone, slashed by the hard emotion which contorted that handsome face. 'What do you mean, fed the fish? He can't even see the damn things!'

'No, but he can hear.' Crockery rattled as she came around the table, knocking against it as anger propelled her forward. 'He can smell. He can feel. Most of all, Blaine, he can feel!'

With her eyes fixed on his in angry challenge, she made to sweep past him then, into the house.

'What do you know about feelings?' His taunting words behind her brought her to a standstill. She glanced back at him, her eyes fixing on his with painful intensity.

There was raw emotion in his face, so tangible she wanted to reach up and touch his cheek, to fling her arms around his neck and cry against the hard cushion of his shoulder that she knew everything there was to know about feelings. That they had wrung her heart and her mind and her soul until she'd thought she would die from the pain of them. But all she said quietly in response to his taunt was, 'More than you could ever imagine, Blaine.'

'But you're too cowardly to face them, aren't you? Aren't you?' he emphasised harshly, because she had turned and was moving away again. 'Is that why you spend your life running away from me?'

Now she couldn't have moved if she had wanted to. Her feet seemed rooted to the cool tiles, so that all she could do was stand there and take his hard castigation as inexorably, behind her, he went on, 'Thirteen years ago! Last time I was here! Now!' A loose tile rocked underfoot as he moved closer to her, causing tension to straighten the tapering triangle of her back. 'What are you running away from, Lydia?' She could feel his warm breath stirring the gentle layering of her hair just above the nape of her neck. 'Your own conscience?' A pause, and then, so quietly that she wasn't even sure she heard him correctly, he breathed, 'Desire?'

Her own breath came like a dragging sensation through her lungs, and her heart started beating as though she were running a marathon.

'If you think that,' she said, half turning, allowing her gaze to lift no further than the middle of his dark, striped tie, 'then you obviously need reminding. What was between us is finished.' How could it hurt so much even now to say it? 'Over with a long time ago.'

She would have moved back inside then if he hadn't prevented it, halting her progress with his raggedly rasped, 'Like hell!'

She sank her teeth into her lower lip, tasted blood upon her tongue.

'You don't know what you're saying,' she uttered in a small voice. He couldn't. He couldn't even guess!

'Don't I?' The touch of his hands on her shoulders sent a surge of panic through her blood, bringing hers to clamp hard onto the taut muscles of his upper arms beneath the immaculate jacket.

'Blaine, please...'

Surprisingly, he hadn't even tried to pull her towards him, his only intention to force her to face him, probably, she thought, to get her to accept the unspeakable truth.

Suddenly, though, she was being released, and realised why as she heard Tina coming out from inside.

'Excuse me.' The girl's discretion was a credit to her, Lydia decided absently, through a tumult of emotion, when Tina moved over to the table without looking at them. At that moment, though, all her mind could fully register was Blaine, looking as tense and distracted as she knew she must look herself.

'By the way, my mother's arriving in Bermuda this morning,' he said, in a voice which, in spite of that episode a moment ago, was surprisingly prosaic.

'Yes, Liam mentioned it.' There was a tremor even in that attempt at normal conversation.

'She's docking in Hamilton this morning,' he went on to inform her. 'I promised we'd be there to pick her up.'

We? Lydia cleared her throat. She was still trembling from that innocent though devastating contact with him a moment ago. 'Does she…know I'm here?' she asked hesitantly, awkwardly aware of Tina clearing the breakfast dishes.

'No. When I last saw her—the day she left New York—I didn't know you were coming.' He, too, she realised, was speaking with that note of reserve so that Tina might believe that they were just polite strangers. Not two people torn apart by a situation that had been contrived and calculated. Not two people with a past…

'She's been under par for some time,' he went on to tell her then, lifting one dark-sleeved arm to the doorjamb in a casual, almost relaxed way. 'She took my father's death hard and we decided that the best thing for her was a holiday. But don't worry.' He grimaced, obviously wise to her unease over the woman finding her there. 'I'm sure she'll be far too prudent to embarrass you with anything you might find…uncomfortable.' His voice was so soft that the clink of crockery behind him almost drowned out those last words.

As he had intended it would, she thought, both powerless and too disconcerted at that moment, with the other girl standing there, to do anything but take his flaying censure as it fell on her ears alone.

Although Bermuda was only twenty-one miles long, and no more than two miles across at its widest point—as Blaine informed her later when they were travelling westward towards the city—the island's narrow winding roads and scenic lanes made the drive to Hamilton seem a relatively long one.

Being a British colony, its traffic moved on the left. But there was nothing British, Lydia decided, in the way the sun blazed down out of a brilliant blue sky, making the lime-washed rooftops of every building, from the houses to the churches and the shops, dazzle like freshly fallen snow.

Cottages lay along the hills beyond the palm-fringed road—pastel pink, blue, green and sunshine-yellow, while modern and Colonial-style mansions—windows winking in the sun—gazed down upon private bays of the most unbelievable blue.

'Oh, look!' Before Lydia could stop it, the cry of delight escaped her, and she leaned forward to watch, hand resting on the head-restraint of the front seat, as dozens of pink crabs—playing dangerous games with their lives—scuttled across the road in front of the Mercedes and disappeared over the nearside bank. Then the import of her words registered with embarrassing regret because of Liam sitting there beside her.

Blaine was driving today, having given Simon the day

off, and now Lydia sensed the silent understanding behind those dark lenses as his eyes met hers in the driver's rearview mirror.

'Those Boilers are six miles long.' He must have noticed where her agitated gaze had strayed to the stretch of bubbling white surf breaking over the reef beyond the turquoise shallows of the ocean. 'Down there. That's Horseshoe Bay—reputed to be one of the most photographed beaches in the world.'

He was making it easy on her, talking casually, glossing over her thoughtless indiscretion of a few moments before.

'It's beautiful,' she agreed, her eyes following the sweeping crescent of coral-pink sand until it disappeared behind the trees and yuccas growing alongside the road. 'But you can't capture Bermuda on camera—I've decided!' She laughed easily then, taking his lead. 'How could you describe to anyone who hasn't been here the sound the lizards and the tree-frogs make at night? And the smells in this place!'

'Scents,' Blaine corrected with an absent smile, applying a sudden, light pressure to the brake as a scooter overtook them and cut in, taking a chance, its speed in excess of the mandatory twenty-two-miles-an-hour speed limit in force all over the island.

'All right, then, scents.' She took his mock reproof with affable grace. 'But just smell it! That air!' Through the car's open window she inhaled its fragrant sweetness. 'The sea! The frangipani!'

'It's oleander,' Liam chipped in automatically, his sense of smell keener than hers, much more acute, compensating for the sight he had lost.

'Thank you, Liam.' She touched his bare forearm in

a friendly gesture, felt its warmth, but wasn't too surprised when he shrank away.

He'd obviously forgotten himself for a moment with that unintended contribution, and now he was just saving face in front of his father, she was astute enough to realise.

Glancing at the mirror again, she was aware of those grey eyes resting on her, catching them off-guard, so that she had time to notice and wonder at the emotion she knew was clouding their depths—that put a slight furrow between his brows above those dark glasses—before he glanced swiftly away.

When they reached Hamilton, Blaine parked the car in a side-street, from where it was only a couple of blocks to the quay.

'Didn't you and Liam manage to get here while I was away?' Blaine enquired, clearly aware of her taking in her surroundings as he locked the car and pocketed the keys. He already knew that this was her first time on the island.

She shook her head, eyes bright with a pleasure she hadn't expected to feel. 'I never imagined it would be anything like this!' she admitted with a smile.

Even here, colour dominated in the bright colonial buildings—offices, hotels and shops—all with the unique stepped roofs which for her, Lydia decided now, would always be one of the most memorable features of Bermuda. But it was the sight, as they moved out of the side-street, of the two huge cruise-liners that really took her breath away, anchored in the blue waters of the harbour, towering, as they did, above the shops and verandah-decked cafés opposite, along the main Front Street of the capital.

'Docks are supposed to be grimy, uninteresting places!' But nothing was grimy or untidy about this lovely city, and she wasn't sure whether it was the sun bouncing off white roofs that made everything appear so clean and pristine, or whether it was simply the Bermudians' pride in their country that ensured that everything looked as if it had just been painted, or scrubbed and polished for the discerning visitor.

Heat rose from the tarmac as the three of them negotiated the busy road across to the quay.

The three of them...

For a moment, with Liam between her and Blaine, she looked over the boy's dark head to the proud, lean lines of his father's profile, and something gave a twist beneath her ribs.

There had been a time—heaven knew how many lifetimes ago—when she had imagined...

Imagined what? That she would have Blaine's child?

A car horn blared. The clip-clop of a horse's hooves intruded on the chaos of her thoughts with the grind of rough wheels over the tarmac. Distractedly she saw the laughing faces in the open carriage as it passed, a mode of transport reserved for tourists, blending with the colour and traditions and the bustle of modern-day Bermuda.

'What are you trying to do? Commit suicide?' She started as a masculine hand pulled her deftly back onto the pavement. 'I think I should be leading *you*—not Liam.'

She smiled weakly, still ravaged by her thoughts, by

the touch of that surprisingly caring hand on her bare arm.

'Are you all right?' Concern lent a sudden gravity to his features.

'I'm fine,' she uttered, quick to reassure him. Only she wasn't.

That moment of weakness—remembering—had sapped her emotional energy, without the added dread of facing his mother.

Without any hint, however, of the turmoil going on inside of her, and with Liam holding her arm, she allowed Blaine to guide them alongside the ship.

Ropes tethered the great liner to the quayside. The eyes of what seemed like a thousand cabins rose, layer upon layer, to the fluttering coloured flags and the onlookers leaning on the rail of the promenade deck, beneath the bright blue canvas of the sky.

As they reached the disembarkation point, Lydia felt as though her stomach muscles were being wrung.

She wished she was somewhere else. Anywhere but here, with this man who despised her without even knowing the facts, from whom she had run away before rather than face with the truth.

She wished she had told him. This morning. The other day when she had first arrived in Bermuda. Explained why she had behaved as she had when she was, after all, just a tortured teenager. Only she hadn't.

And that's just your own stupid fault, she berated herself, deciding that all she could do now was brazen it out with Judith Caldwell.

But those hidden anxieties, which she would never

have let Blaine see, refused to be quashed by her outward show of bravado. Consequently, she appeared pale and taciturn several minutes later when they met his mother off the ship.

CHAPTER FIVE

JUDITH CALDWELL was just as Lydia remembered her. Tall and slim, with that air of pure detachment about her that promised that no matter how ruffled or perturbed others might become around her, she would remain cool and above it all. Her hair was greyer now, though, and the dark smudges beneath her eyes gave some indication as to the depth of her grief over her recent widowhood.

'Mother.' Blaine's greeting was a mere peck on Judith's cheek. Probably all that this rather aloof woman would demand or expect, Lydia decided, as Blaine tipped the smart young steward who had carried Judith's luggage to the quayside.

Lydia watched her embrace her grandson, who surprisingly was allowing himself to be hugged. But now, as that grey head lifted and turned in her direction, Lydia's stomach muscles contracted queasily.

That curious smile the woman had turned her way was being replaced by shock. Shock which she was too well-mannered to actually express, only in a subtle lifting of her brows.

'Mrs Caldwell.' It was all Lydia could do to acknowledge Blaine's mother, wondering, as she was, what the woman was thinking.

'Mother.' Mercifully, before Judith could utter a word, Blaine was intervening. 'I believe you know Lydia. Lydia Lawrence.'

A small shudder travelled down Lydia's spine. Why

did it sound cheap? Thick with notoriety? Even to herself?

'Of course.' And that refined voice of Judith's, with that uneasy smile, assured Lydia that she wasn't the only one who thought so. Clearly the mother of the man she had supposedly so cruelly jilted hadn't forgotten. But good manners prevailed even in spite of that, prompting the woman to enquire, 'How are you, dear?'

It was a perfunctory question, asked merely for something to say, and therefore Lydia treated it as such as she returned an equally forced smile.

'It's nice to see you again.' It was as mechanical a response as Judith's had been, Lydia thought, feeling like a hypocrite, because it wasn't nice. It was farcical— for all of them. And now, against the backdrop of the great liner that had brought Blaine's mother safely from New York, she saw the woman send a rather baffled glance up at her son.

'I didn't realise that you two…were—' She broke off, looking slightly awkward, too reserved, too tactful to actually say it.

'We're not.' Above the hum of the city traffic, Lydia caught Blaine's positive denial. 'Purely coincidental, Mother,' he assured her laconically. Only it wasn't, Lydia thought. Because Heather had taken it on herself to arrange it, hadn't she?

Nevertheless, beneath her cream, short-sleeved blouse and burgundy voile skirt, the woman appeared to relax a little.

'You look so young. You'll have to tell me your secret, Lydia,' Blaine's mother complimented, weighing up the chic dark hair and clear, cosmetic-free skin, the flattering sage-green of her top and matching shorts that emphasised her lean, lithe fitness—saying the right thing. 'And do call me Judith.'

Silently, Lydia applauded the woman for her discretion. She must have been dying to ask all sorts of questions. But Blaine was right. Those impeccable manners would never have allowed her to voice them.

With a measure of gratitude, Lydia stooped to pick up a piece of Judith's luggage.

'Leave that.'

As her hand reached for the handle of the one piece of hand luggage so did Blaine's, and she stepped swiftly back, leaving him to it, her breath catching as though she had touched a live element.

Out of the corner of her eye she noticed the calculating glance his mother directed at her. But all the woman said was, 'Liam. Come. Take my arm, and you can tell me what you've been doing since you arrived.'

Still struggling for composure, Lydia was surprised to see the boy looking past his grandmother, his dark brows knitted as he searched sightlessly—and for *her,* she realised, touched.

'Go ahead, Liam,' she murmured amiably. 'She's come a long way to see you.'

Therefore the boy did as he was told, while Blaine, his mother's small vanity case dangling from one hand, picked up the one remaining suitcase and started leading them back to the car.

'What is it about you that even a recalcitrant adolescent responds to, Lydia?'

His query was chastening and unexpected as they were passing the second of the great liners anchored there beside the quay. In his pale Bermudas and matching knee-high socks he looked like a typical islander, yet supremely imposing and confident.

Lydia glanced back, noticing that the other two had stopped beside the horse-drawn carriages that were standing under a canopy beside the busy road. One of the Bermudian drivers, smart in white hat and shorts, was chatting good-humouredly to them as Judith guided her grandson's hand to pet the warm muzzle of one of the trusting animals.

Lydia turned back, emotion clogging her throat.

'Who knows? Maybe I do have some redeeming qualities, Blaine,' she tried to advise him lightly, her smile wry, her eyes concealed behind the dark lenses of her sunglasses.

'Do you?' Though his own eyes were shielded, she knew the look he gave her was hard and sceptical as they came to a standstill beside a pelican crossing. 'What I wouldn't have given to have caught one glimpse of one thirteen years ago.'

Thirteen years ago? Before he had married Sharon?

Lydia's thoughts raced as she dragged her gaze from the hard power of his body to stare absently at the traffic moving past.

Tourer-type taxis, reflecting the sun in their gleaming white paintwork. Hatchbacks with their rear doors gaping wide so as to circulate the hot, humid air. Scooters buzzed past, many ridden by tourists—Americans mainly—unused to driving on the left, while others wove in and out, manoeuvred easily by the native Bermudians who rode then, often one-handed, with a devil-may-care type of casualness.

'You will not tell anyone of this…indiscretion. You will leave now—and no one will know.' Flooding back across the years, she heard her prospective father-in-law's soft, emotionless command. 'I'll arrange everything…'

Everything to swiftly evict her from Blaine's life. Because it had been he who arranged for Blaine to discover what an opportunist he had been about to marry. He who had arranged for the more than willing Jeremy Tyndall to back up the story that she was having an affair with him. He who had arranged for her to be caught by Blaine with the more easily bought newspaper baron.

As sightlessly as Liam's, her eyes were fixed on the lively, brightly coloured shops on the other side of the road, with their endless display of T-shirts and paintings and touristy knick-knacks. But she saw only the picture of Blaine's face when he had burst into the party at Tyndall's house that fateful night, seen her in his arms, dancing with him, and she shuddered.

'Perhaps Liam takes me as I am—and not for what he thinks I am,' she murmured sadly, and was repaid only by a sceptical grunt before the lights changed to admit them across the busy road.

That afternoon they had a picnic on the beach. Not either of the private beaches that adjoined the house, but a small cove not too far away below the lush slopes of what Blaine described to Lydia as the world's finest golf course, and she could see why.

Its manicured greens and fairways spread away on either side of the road, its undulating slopes and flower-hedged valleys offering both a challenge and an escape that was a golf enthusiast's dream.

But it was the cove, arrived at by steps leading down onto soft pink sand, that caused her to gasp with wonder.

Here the surf, pounding for centuries against the caves along the island's south shore, had sculpted what Blaine informed her were known as the Natural Arches, spectacular rock formations framing the near-deserted beach and the turquoise ocean.

They had a snack of fresh lobster, rolls and salad and white wine—with fruit juice for Liam—spread out on a cloth on the warm sand. And afterwards, with Judith engrossed in a book with her back against the rocks and Blaine relaxing, his long body stretched out on one of the dark blue towels, Lydia grabbed the ball that he had brought for Liam from one of the carrier bags and invited the boy to join her in a game.

It was a special ball, with a bell inside to enable Liam to locate it by sound alone. And he was as swift as she was, if not swifter, at getting to it, she marvelled when they were involved in a light-hearted game of football, his face flushed, his adolescent laughter ringing over hers as he leaped to the ball now and gave it a particularly hard kick towards the foaming surf.

'Is this a private club or can anyone join?'

Blaine was beside them, his dark features softened with amusement.

'It's exclusive,' Lydia teased, warming automatically to his smile. 'As exclusive as that golf club you pointed out to us. And I bet you're a member of that!'

Wry lines pulled at his mouth. 'That sounds like an accusation,' he remarked, stooping to catch the ball as it raced in on the surging tide. And as he stood up again, tall and bronzed in nothing but dark bathing trunks, with the timeless rocks behind him, the sheer perfection of him produced a kick of something unbearable deep down inside Lydia, something that shook her with a strength as fierce as her efforts to deny it. 'Well, are you going to let me play?'

She was glad of the diversion, forcing herself to be aware of other things. Like the hot sun playing down across her slickly oiled shoulders and back exposed by the skimpy green Lycra bikini, like the damp sand, oozing, like soft warm cream, between her toes.

'What do you think, Liam? Shall we let him?' she pretended to deliberate, laughing down at Blaine's son.

Less rebellious than usual where his father was concerned, Liam gave an uncaring little shrug. 'If he wants to,' he accepted noncommittally.

'I see. So one has to have the backing of all members first, does one?' Blaine grinned, tossing the ball into the air. He caught it, twirling it on his index finger with the skill of a master.

'Yes, and I'm hopeless at ball games so Liam and I are nearly evenly matched,' Lydia informed him. 'But if *you* play he's never going to have a chance.'

She stooped to whisper something to Liam, who gave a loud whoop of laughter.

'What's the joke?' Those grey eyes looking down at her from that strong tanned face were decidedly circumspect.

'We've decided that you're going to have to wear a blindfold,' she declared mischievously.

'You're kidding?' He looked positively aghast.

'No, I'm not. It's fair,' she laughed.

'In that case, so will you.'

'No problem.'

Bashing the ball out of his hand, she charged, laughing, up the beach, returning with two of the large white napkins from the carrier containing the remnants of their picnic, having prompted an amused remark from Judith.

In fact the blindfolds gave them at least some idea of how important sounds were to someone who was severely sight impaired, Lydia decided a little later, when they were being guided by each other's laughter and the bell in the wayward ball as someone, probably Blaine, she thought, from the sound of that hefty kick, aimed it across the sand.

Blindly, she ran towards it, and heard it being kicked back before she could get her bearings.

'This isn't fair!' she laughed after several attempts to kick it were foiled by either the sharper senses or the quicker reflexes of the two males.

'You were the one who said it was!' From somewhere behind her she heard Blaine's smug laughter, and could just make out the low tones of people talking, somewhere, she guessed, near the arches in the spectacular rocks.

The sea was on her right. She could hear its interminable surge and retreat, and through it suddenly she caught the faint ring of the ball again.

She ran towards it, guided only by the sound, feeling the caress of the water, like rivulets of silk over her feet, as one especially powerful and errant wave coursed over the sand. And suddenly she tripped, her arms coming out in front of her to save herself as, in the next instant, she collided with something decidedly solid and warm.

Startled, she felt the bulge of hard muscle and crisp body hair as she tumbled breathlessly onto the coral bed beneath the shallow water, the steadying masculine hand on her shoulder and the arm around her bare midriff, shocking and warm.

Hectically, she pulled off her blindfold and saw Blaine's eyes laughing down at her. Swiftly then, she tried to get up, only to find herself pinned by a hair-roughened thigh lying heavily across hers.

'Well, well. It's been a long time, hasn't it?' The rawness of his voice belied the humour in his eyes, trembling with a sensuality she remembered.

'Let me go, Blaine.' Her own voice cracked from the panic evoked by their tangled limbs, dark bronze intertwined with palest gold. She put her hands behind her to try and prise his arm from around her waist, the action causing her golden breasts to swell above the skimpy green top of her bikini.

'Why? I wasn't aware this was always such anathema to you.' All humour had left him now. 'After what we were…'

'What we were?' Something quivered through her voice, and an emotion nearing panic darkened the deep sapphire of her eyes. 'What were we? We weren't anything!' she stressed fiercely over the relentless surge of the ocean. 'At least…not lovers. We were never lovers!' She decried it with a vehemence bordering on the desperate, causing those black brows to come together in a puzzled frown.

Those grey eyes fixed on hers with a studious intensity, their regard of her analytical and eternal.

'Of course not,' he acceded eventually with the barest inclination of his head. 'Forgive me for even intimating otherwise.' In spite of what he had said, though, his tone begged no forgiveness. 'You would never *consciously* commit yourself to letting it happen, would you? Not with me, at any rate. Just with every other man that came after me!'

His words struck her like the force of the wave that rushed in behind her off the inky horizon, rocking her forward so that it was only those strong hands on her shoulders now that kept their upper bodies from actually touching.

'Do you want to know the truth?' she flung at him, her nostrils flaring as she prepared to hit him with it.

But all he said thickly was, 'Save it, Lydia,' and got up and waded out of the water, back to Liam, who was calling them from some way up the beach.

Thwarted in her efforts to defend herself, Lydia wandered back to where Judith still sat reading beneath a wide-brimmed floppy hat, dropping down onto one of the beach towels.

'You seemed to be enjoying yourself out there with Liam, Lydia. And my son.'

Stretching out on the towel, Lydia tensed, noting that somewhat derogatory note in the way she had referred to Blaine. But what could she expect? she asked herself reasonably. With Judith believing the worst about her as she obviously did.

'Yes, Liam's not a bad kiddie,' she remarked, steering the conversation onto a safer course as she lay, eyes closed against the hard rays of the sun.

She heard Judith's sharp inhalation. 'That's as may be, but it isn't Liam I'm concerned about.'

Shielding her eyes with one hand, Lydia turned her head to glance up at her.

'Oh?' This line of conversation was disconcerting and unexpected, putting a fine line between Lydia's dark brows.

'I hope you won't misunderstand me when I…say I wish you hadn't come here.'

Lydia caught her breath, only the soft rise of her breasts and the tightening of her flat stomach revealing the increasing tension in the slender lines of her body.

'I know Blaine said it was a total accident that you were here at all.' Had he? So Judith must have pressed him, Lydia thought, as the woman went on, 'But it's inadvisable for you to stay. I'd rather you went home.'

She couldn't have put it more bluntly if she had tried!

Lydia's throat worked nervously. This was truly out of character for Judith, she realised, conscious of how concerned for Blaine the woman must be for her to have said it at all.

'You've no need to worry,' she assured Judith, propping herself up on an elbow. 'I can assure you I've got no designs on your son.'

He had just emerged from the blue water, and was wading up to where Liam lay basking in the shallow waves. His soaked hair gleamed like jet under the late afternoon sun, while rivulets coursed down his body, matting the dark hair of his chest and powerful legs.

'That isn't how it appears to me. I've seen the way you look at him—the way he looks at you. Blaine was hurt badly before and I don't want him hurt again. He's been through enough.'

Meaning with losing Sharon and Liam's accident, Lydia deduced.

'I told you—you don't have to worry,' she breathed, and, with a determination that took some enforcing, 'Blaine means nothing to me any more.'

Judith made a wry sound down her nostrils. 'It isn't only your feelings that concern me, Lydia. Look at you.'

Almost disapprovingly, her gaze ran over Lydia's thick, chicly cut dark hair, the enviable bone structure of her face and the still model-slim lines of her well-proportioned figure. 'No man would be a man if he wasn't attracted to you. If you've any heart at all, you'll do what's best for all of us and get right away from here. Apart from which, I think it's only fair to tell you that for the first time since Sharon died he's starting to get seriously involved with someone else.'

Blaine came up to them then, leading Liam, and so as not to face him, with a heart like lead, Lydia flopped back down on her towel—though not before noticing Judith smile at both her son and grandson as though nothing had happened.

The following night, Blaine hosted a dinner party at the house. It was, Lydia decided, a small gathering, with guests chosen primarily by Judith, since several of them seemed to be friends she had known in England who had moved to Bermuda for occupational reasons and had now made this beautiful island their retirement home.

One guest, though, Lydia realised at once, hadn't arrived solely for Judith's benefit.

Shelley Graham was a Bermudian-born blonde with a rather too curvy figure and a tendency, whenever she spoke to Liam—who, with Lydia, had been invited to join them for dinner—to shout at him as though he was deaf as well as blind.

Lacking any real beauty, Shelley more than made up for it, Lydia discovered, with a hard-edged intelligence that had earned her an enviable position as one of Blaine's top financial consultants. And, with an unreasonable emotion to which she refused even to put a name, Lydia knew that this was the woman Judith had been referring to when she had mentioned Blaine becoming seriously involved with someone.

'So you have the thankless task of being Liam's nanny,' Shelley commented to Lydia after Liam had been excused and gone upstairs.

They were lingering over coffee in the elaborate dining room, a relaxed mix of elderly men smoking cigars while their wives chatted to Judith. Blaine was at the cocktail bar, pouring drinks.

'I wouldn't say it was thankless, Shelley,' Lydia countered with a cursory glance at the empty chair beside her, immediately across the table from the disparaging blonde. 'I find it very rewarding.'

Shelley's mouth compressed in what Lydia could only construe as a rather belittling smile, one eyebrow lifting, pale as her hair which she wore combed back from her forehead in an immaculate French pleat.

'You must be a masochist,' she breathed. She sipped her brandy through bright red lips that matched the talon-like nails around her glass and a scarlet dress that Lydia couldn't help thinking made her full figure look shrink-wrapped. Gold jewellery gleamed with every movement. In her own simple black dress, with its thin straps, and the silver torque she wore at her throat to complement small silver earrings, she felt comfortably pleased with her own taste.

But now the woman, glass raised beside her cheek, was studying her with the same mixture of pensiveness and curiosity with which she had been looking at her all evening, and suddenly, with her green eyes narrowing, she asked, 'Weren't you Lydia Lawrence?'

Lydia tensed, aware that everyone else had stopped

talking. Blaine had only introduced her to them all as Lydia, Liam's nanny.

'I still am,' she returned with unashamed dignity, shooting an unconscious glance at Blaine.

Dark as Satan, in black trousers and a rather loose creamy shirt, he was coming back with the liqueurs, and she knew he had heard, but he looked totally unperturbed. Perhaps he had just been trying to spare *her* any embarrassment by not introducing her fully, she thought, surprised.

She felt the atmosphere become a little strained, felt that sudden recognition that showed in everyone's eyes—connecting her with the old lifestyle that no one who read a daily newspaper would ever quite forget—and she knew what they all had to be thinking. What was the woman who had thrown Blaine Caldwell over for another man doing here looking after his child?

'I thought your face was familiar.' Rather too loudly Shelley's voice cut through the awkward silence. 'Blaine, you are a dark horse! Fancy not telling us you'd be entertaining a celebrity!'

Lydia's smile was less than sincere as she averted her eyes from the disturbing intensity of Blaine's to murmur nonetheless politely, 'A celebrity, Shelley? Hardly. Not any more.'

'Yes, they say the life of a model is phenomenally short, don't they?' the other woman persisted, resentment obvious in the glittering green of her eyes. 'I mean, physical perfection can't last for ever, can it?'

'Can't it, Shelley?' Above the rattle of a spoon in its saucer and the murmurs of thanks from the two men being handed drinks by Blaine, Lydia felt a surge of dangerous warmth pulse through her as she realised that his compliment was being aimed at her. 'It's in the eye of the beholder, after all.'

'Isn't it?' Shelley emphasised, with a knowing, side-long glance at him that didn't fail to notice where he was looking, but her laughter was a little too high-pitched, too strained. 'Seriously, though, it's got to be easier coping with being plain and fat, with only a per-sonality to rely on.' Her comments were directed solely at Lydia now. 'You know. What you've never had, you never miss. Rather than have the perfect face and figure and be aware all the time that some day you're going to lose it. That must be very hard on women in your pro-fession.'

If the remark had come from anyone else, Lydia might have found herself having to agree that with some mod-els she had known the obsession with losing their looks *had* made their lives a total misery. But she didn't feel inclined to lay open the emotional problems of what, after all, had been old contemporaries and friends with a woman like Shelley Graham. Neither had she liked the rather derogatory way in which the woman had em-phasised that last bit about women in her 'profession'. It was a further dig at her own unfounded notoriety, Lydia felt. And, succinctly now, she responded with, 'We cope.'

After that, one of the older women caught Shelley's attention, and, having had enough of her snipes for one night, Lydia excused herself on the justifiable grounds of attending to Liam.

She caught Blaine's slicing glance as she got up from the table but chose to ignore it, and, finding the door open on to the front porch as she was heading for the stairs, she slipped outside into the scented night.

Wildlife whistled around her, its familiar shrill song emanating from every tree and exotic shrub hemming the front lawn. And then, above it, on the still of the air, she heard the deep, rich resonance of Blaine's voice just behind her. 'I'm sorry about that.'

He meant what had just happened inside—with Shelley—and her chest lifted deeply before she answered.

'Are you?' She sent a guarded glance back at him over her shoulder. 'I would have thought you'd think it was no less than I deserved.'

'Would you?' His shoes made a soft sound on the ground as he moved towards her. 'Then you don't know me very well, Lydia.'

There was nothing seductive in that sentence. Why, then, was her heart thumping? Her senses locking up to protect her from that familiar, very lethal brand of charm?

'Is that why you didn't tell them who I really was?'

He was standing beside her now, his vital presence a threat to her peace of mind, her wavering equilibrium. 'Would you have preferred it if they had known?'

She turned away from him, staring at a new moon hanging above the dark crown of the poinciana tree.

'Only in so far as it would have spared Shelley from having to make rather a fool of herself in her unspoken yet very obvious claim to you!'

She thought she heard him chuckle under his breath. 'You're very benevolent,' he said softly, but made no disclaimer of Shelley's proprietorial rights.

She laughed to pretend she didn't care. 'Don't accuse me of that!'

'I wasn't.'

Of course. He knew her better than anyone, didn't he? Or he thought he did.

'Blaine…' She pivoted to face him, suddenly unable to bear it any longer. She would tell him now. Get it over with. And to hell with the consequences. They were something he—and, yes, Judith too—would have to work out for themselves. 'Blaine, you've got to list—'

A finger on her lips shocked her into silence, its sensual implication paralysing.

'No confessions,' he said. 'They don't become you, Lydia.'

'How do you know?' she challenged as his hand fell away from her, leaving her breathing fast and shallowly. 'Do you think I'm the only one capable of any wrongdoing, while your own family are so blameless? Weren't you even angry with your father for trying to buy me off?'

'Trying?' In the light that spilled from the open door she could see the scepticism graven on those masculine features.

'Weren't you?' she enquired brittly, refusing to be sidetracked into an argument with him.

He made a derisive sound down his nostrils. 'I was only glad it stopped me from making a gross error of judgement,' he said, his words flaying her raw.

And instead he had made his very acceptable match with Sharon.

'Bravo for you, then!' she uttered, pretending it hadn't hurt.

As she made to flounce away, headed back inside, he swung after her, taking her unawares as he caught her wrist, stalling her precipitate flight.

'Lydia.'

She sucked in her breath, and put all her senses on hold again. 'Yes.' It was barely audible, lost in the dangerous darkness.

'I don't want to quarrel with you.'

Oh, God! His voice was too soft, too deep, too warm.

'What are you saying?' Her breath trembled through her lungs. 'You want us to be friends?' She looked at him warily, feeling his thumb tracing the pumping blue vein in her wrist with a devastation that left her floundering.

'I don't think we can ever be that,' he murmured with unstinting truth.

No. Not friends. Not lovers either! Something inside her shrieked its cruel insistent warning. She couldn't bear it if he was kind to her, if he showed her any tenderness. She'd rather have him cruel and bitter, throwing insults at her. At least she could cope with that.

'I'm your employee, Blaine. That's all,' she reminded him, with her chin coming up to add conviction to her forced indifference, but it took every ounce of willpower she possessed to walk away from him, back to the house.

Already in his pyjamas, Liam was sitting up in bed, listening to his Walkman when Lydia looked in.

'I hate Shelley Graham,' he started with childlike honesty when he realised Lydia was there. Sulkily he tossed his earphones down onto the bedspread. 'She speaks to me ever so slowly—like I'm stupid or something. I hope Dad doesn't marry her. I'm never going to let her take the place of my mother.'

'No one can do that, Liam,' Lydia assured him, putting the discarded Walkman on his bedside cabinet. 'Nor would your father expect them to. People can't be replaced like belongings.' Didn't she know better than anyone how true that was? And then casually, unable to stop herself as she straightened the boy's bedspread, she murmured, 'I suppose your father loved your mother very much.'

Liam lifted a nonchalant shoulder. 'Yeah, I guess he did.'

Something gave a little twist inside of her before she steeled herself to ask, 'Did they get on well?'

'Not always. They quarrelled sometimes. They were quarrelling on the day Mum had her accident. That's why she drove off like she did.'

Lydia plumped up his pillows, suddenly feeling like an eavesdropper. 'Perhaps you shouldn't be telling me this, Liam.'

'It's OK.' He shrugged again and slid further down into the bed, propping himself up on an elbow. 'I think they were quarrelling over someone Dad used to know. I overheard. A tramp. Mum found a photograph of her in Dad's study, but she didn't look very poor to me. She was sitting in a super-duper sportscar.' Sightlessly his eyes sought the approximate position of Lydia's. 'How would Dad know a tramp?' he asked, frowning.

She shivered as though someone had touched her with icy fingers. Dear Liam. For all his being forced to mature, he was still naive, still very much a child.

A photograph of a woman. 'A tramp', Liam had called her. Lydia Lawrence. Super-tramp. She was glad the boy couldn't see the anguished question she knew was burning in her eyes.

If what he was saying was true, then that likeness could have been one of the last things he had seen before the accident that had robbed him of his sight. Her like-ness, in all probability.

No. Certainty, she thought with cold, gut-wrenching assurance, because hadn't Blaine snapped her once when she'd had the Porsche? And Liam had said his mother had driven off as she had because she had been quar-relling with Blaine over...

Over what? Over *her?* she wondered harrowingly. Because if that was the case, then did that mean that she was responsible for Sharon Caldwell's death? For Liam being blind?

She had to give a conscious shake of her head to rid herself of the torturous thoughts that were suddenly stalking through her brain, and it took every ounce of composure she possessed to say, 'I don't think your mother meant that sort of tramp, Liam.'

The boy's frown merely deepened.

'When you're a bit older you'll understand what she meant.'

He sat up then, his eyes widening as though he were suddenly willing them to see.

'Do you mean like someone...not very nice?' he asked, excitement colouring his voice.

Lydia felt something like an unbearable weight press-ing down on her chest. Even coming innocently, as it was from Liam, it still had the power to hurt.

'Do you remember what she looked like?' she asked, sitting down on the edge of the bed. She had to know for sure. She had to!

Liam bit his lip, that thick hair falling forward as he shook his head. 'I think she had very long black hair.'

Of course. Hadn't she asked for that? Nevertheless, Liam's words seemed to sap all of her strength.

She reached for his hand and very slowly drew it upwards to cup her cheek.

'Did she look anything like me?'

He ran his fingers over her face, employing both hands to the curve of her high cheekbones, the straight nose and full mouth and the softly contoured chin that made up her famous bone structure.

'I don't know,' he confessed, sounding frustrated. 'But yesterday—on the beach—I asked Dad what you looked like.'

Lydia caught her breath, and was unable to prevent herself from asking, 'What did he say?'

'He said you were very beautiful.'

She turned her head aside, staring at the bedside lamp she had switched on for her own benefit, glad that he had finished his tactile inspection so that he wouldn't detect the tears that were doing their level best to spill out onto her cheeks.

'How did you know my dad?'

Liam's unexpected question brought her head round. Of course. She had told him that first day that she had known Blaine a long time ago.

'We met at a press launch. That's what they call a party for the start of an advertising campaign. I was a model and I'd made a series of commercials for a company which was one of your father's clients. I had to be there as I was the main person promoting their product, and your father had been invited because of his involvement with the financial affairs. That's where we first met.'

'Before he met my mother?'

'No,' she answered. Sharon Hillier had always been there—the daughter of another famous name in the financial world. She remembered how resentfully the other girl had viewed her when she'd turned up with Blaine once at one of his company's functions. 'No,' she said again, 'but before he'd decided to marry her.' God! How it hurt to say it. But ultimately, of course, when he had, it had been a marriage not just of two people but of two great businesses.

'Did he ask you to marry him?'

So many questions! she thought, as Liam's latest hit her right out of the blue, but she felt compelled to answer.

'Yes. He asked me to marry him.'

'Then why didn't you?'

Deserving of the truth though he was, Lydia couldn't answer that openly even now.

'Some things aren't meant to be,' she said gently, and couldn't resist giving him a peck on the forehead before getting to her feet.

'Why not? Didn't you love him?'

She hesitated. What could she say? Twelve-year-old boys didn't talk about love unless it was to sneer at the silliness of it. But this was no ordinary twelve-year-old, and after all he had been through, Lydia considered, this child deserved the truth.

'Yes, I loved him very much.' She said it with every ounce of feeling that was still inside of her for Blaine, that she knew would always be with her.

'Then why didn't you marry him?' he persisted. 'I thought when people fell in love they always got married.'

Yes, she had thought the same, she remembered, with a bitter twist of poignancy—when she was eighteen.

Unsophisticated and unaware of the cruel blow that fate was about to deal her.

'Not always,' she responded, bending to snap off the bedside light. 'Besides, he loved your mother more.'

He had had to, she thought torturously, to have married her like that—so quickly—as though she, Lydia, had never existed.

But what did it matter? she reminded herself savagely after leaving Liam. He could have married a thousand Sharons—or no one at all—and it wouldn't have made a scrap of difference, would it? She, Lydia, was what she was, and Blaine's father had been right to stop her marrying him. As Blaine would have been compelled to do if he'd been told the truth.

CHAPTER SIX

LYDIA lay awake for what seemed like hours, the things Liam had told her revolving round and round her mind— like a top that refused to stop spinning—keeping her wide-eyed, plagued by a myriad questions.

Like was that what Blaine had meant when he'd referred to the grief she had brought to his family? The fact that he and Sharon had been quarrelling over her the day Sharon had died? That the whole tragedy—both Sharon's and Liam's—had been her fault?

In the darkness of her room, a small sob escaped her, lost on the softly whirring blades of the ceiling fan.

But why should she feel so totally to blame? Surely it was hardly her fault, she thought, without any solace whatsoever from her attempted reasoning. And why had Blaine been keeping a photograph of her at all? For a memento? A keepsake? Or had he—in spite of all he had been told—had believed about her—and in spite of being married—still cared?

The possibility that he had—that he might still—filled her with a helpless surge of emotion.

Dear God! If she could only believe that he still... That he didn't hate her...

She bit her lip to stem the wild wave of elation that was coursing through her. What was she doing? Even daring to imagine that he could ever love her as she had believed he had loved her before?

Suddenly elation was tumbling, like the waters of a burst dam, into bitter despair.

Judith was right, she realised wretchedly. She should get away from here. Though Judith's reasons for wanting her to go were entirely different from her own.

Sick at heart, she ripped back her covers and got out of bed, envying those who could find their relaxation in alcohol or even sleep-inducing medication.

She could, however, make use of her insomnia and write to Gary, she thought, slipping a gold, cap-sleeved short negligee over her matching strappy nightdress, and went and sat down at the antique cedar bureau in the other room.

There was headed notepaper, very elegant and very impressive, with its embossed lettering at the top. But for some reason she didn't want to tell Gary that she was working for Blaine Caldwell. He'd known of her involvement with Blaine before, and the consequences she had suffered after their break-up, although she had never told him the reason for it and he, like the treasured friend he was, had never asked.

Therefore, she scribbled a few lines to him on one of the pristine sheets of plain white paper, telling him she was working away for a couple of weeks, that she'd be in touch when she got back, and putting simply 'Bermuda' and the date in the top right-hand corner.

That done, she felt more awake than ever, yet a swift scan of the bookshelf beside the bureau offered nothing that appealed. There were, however, several books she had noticed and made a mental note to look at in the downstairs library.

So why not? she thought, moving back into the other room and grimacing at the rumpled bed. Anything but lie there and torture herself with things she could never change.

The house was quiet, save for the somnolent tick of a clock somewhere in the imposing hall and the soft movement of the bead curtain she had parted with care before her barefooted descent down the stairs.

The library was next to Blaine's study, and, feeling for the door handle, since she hadn't dared put on a light, Lydia turned it very quietly, the unexpected realisation of softly illuminated bookcases and cedar panelling drawing an intrusive little sound from her lips.

'Lydia.' Blaine was already vacating the easy chair he had been lounging in by the open fireplace.

'I—I'm sorry. I didn't realise…' Her apology was so obviously tremulous in the stillness of the dimly lit room.

'What didn't you realise, darling? That there'd be two of us who couldn't sleep?'

Irony touched that beautiful mouth, but there was, she sensed, a lurking tension beneath those casually elegant clothes he had worn at dinner, and with an unconscious flick of her tongue over suddenly dry lips, she apologised again and made to retreat.

'No, don't go.' If that was a request then it was lost in the authority of a cool command. 'Come in and join me. Perhaps we can keep each other company in our mutual insomnia.'

His eyes touched briefly on the softly tanned skin exposed by the gaping gold of her negligee. She felt their caress like that of a warm breeze that was suddenly surging with a dangerous electricity, and in a voice that almost cracked she uttered, 'I don't think that's a very good idea.'

But her feet seemed rooted to the spot, and, with something pulling at his mouth, he said, 'Why not? What can you possibly fear from being alone with me?'

Emotion tightened her throat, clogging her powers of speech as he came over and very purposefully pushed the door closed behind her.

'Why couldn't you sleep, Lydia?' His arm was mere centimetres from her cheek. She could feel his body warmth beneath the immaculate sleeve, smell the faint musk of his skin beneath the lingering traces of his cologne. 'Is your conscience troubling you?'

There was mockery in his voice, but cloaked resentment too and, conscious of being—as he'd said—so alone with him, she moved swiftly past him, over to the easy chairs.

Perhaps he'd hit the right mark, because her conscience was certainly troubling her, she thought. But not for the reasons he was obviously referring to.

She subsided onto the chair opposite the one he had been sitting in.

'That day Sharon died,' she started without preliminaries. 'You were quarrelling over me, weren't you?' She knew she was incriminating Liam but she had to say it.

'Who told you—? He broke off, that dark head nodding in sudden realisation, his lips tightening with something that looked like half-resignation, half-anger.

'So it was my fault that she died. My fault that Liam lost his sight,' she appended, laying bare the fears and implications that had been troubling her all night. Her eyes were trained on the heavy book that Blaine had been reading, discarded on the arm of the chair opposite. A history book. Educational. Mind-improving. 'You were right. It was my fault she had that accident.' She lifted her tortured gaze to his, her perfect features—devoid of any make-up—wan and incredibly youthful. 'It was mine, wasn't it? Not Liam's.'

His breath seemed to leave him in a gush as he took the few strides needed to bring him over to stand in front of her.

'I've never blamed Liam,' he rasped. 'Or you. Believe it or not, whatever I've said, I've never really blamed you. The responsibility's all mine for never being able to get you out of my blood!'

Face tilted to his, her lips parted with incomprehension at what he was saying with so much passion, so much anger.

'But you loved Sharon. You married her...' Her features were wrought with disbelief as she tried to assimilate all that he was saying.

'Yes, I married her,' he breathed. 'But it was a marriage of convenience, and she knew it, but she didn't care as long as she had what she wanted—a child and the merger of our two companies and all that went with it. I would have married anyone,' he admitted roughly. 'After you, I didn't give a damn who I spent my life with. I was through with bleeding hearts and broken promises.'

'So you never loved her?' Her trembling whisper was succeeded by the harsh laugh that sprang from Blaine.

'Love?' A sneer contorted the hard lines of his mouth. 'What did you ever know about love? No, I didn't love her,' he threw at her then. 'Though God knows I did my best to make it work! We were incompatible in every way—except in our mutual affection for Liam—and eventually I grew to be grateful even for that. So don't talk to me about love. You who sold out as soon as you were offered a deal compatible with your scandalous lifestyle!'

'That isn't true!' she defended, and started as the book on the opposite chair suddenly crashed to the floor with a thud. 'I told you the other night...I never accepted that money. He paid it straight into my account. You were right. A draft so that it would clear immediately. But the very next day I took steps to arrange for it all to be sent back to him.'

He had moved closer and was standing, tall and judgemental, above her. 'And you expect me to believe that?'

'Yes.'

'Why?'

'Because it's the truth.'

'The truth.' He seemed to be weighing this for a moment. Then, 'Did Tyndall promise you more?' he queried acidly. 'Is that it?'

'No.'

'What, then?' He looked grim, yet even while he condemned her that special attraction he possessed still had the power to ensnare her with its frightening intensity. 'Were you so in love with him that getting away from me was all that mattered? Is that why you sank into that wild and totally abandoned way of life—because he wouldn't have you? Did you promise him all the things you promised me, only to find yourself on the receiving end of your own treatment?'

His words lanced through her, but she deserved them; she knew she did. She deserved them all. For not telling him...

Fixing her gaze on a softly lit painting of a steamship

at anchor on the panelled wall behind him, she said, 'I never wanted Jeremy Tyndall.' There, it was out. Uttered. Confessed.

'What?' Lines of shocked bewilderment slashed deeply into his face. 'Then why the blazes…?'

Clearly he was having difficulty digesting that piece of information, Lydia thought, and gave a startled gasp as suddenly he dragged her up out of the chair.

'Damn you!' The pressure of his fingers bit into her upper arms as her own hands came up against the sensuality of the fabric covering his chest, desperate to hold him at bay. 'What the devil's that supposed to mean? First you say it wasn't for the money. Now you're telling me it wasn't because of Tyndall. Then why the hell *did* you leave me? Or did you simply fall out of love with me? Is that it? Then if so, say it!' He looked almost savage, those hard hands practically shaking it out of her. 'Tell me you didn't love me! Say it, Lydia!'

'I didn't love you.' The lie burned like acid on her tongue, and she gave a small cry as his arm locked around her, bending her backwards across it.

'Liar! You were as much a victim of your feelings for me as I was for you!'

'Don't!' It was a plea against making her admit things she couldn't possibly admit to him now, against the angry heat of his body and sensations that, with this one man alone, she couldn't allow herself to feel.

What was it going to take? she thought. The truth, to make him draw away from her in sickening revulsion? Because he would be sickened—as he would have been thirteen years ago.

'It can't be, Blaine!' Her lovely face was lined with

the struggle to suppress the dangerous emotions deep inside of her. 'It can never be!'

'Why not?' He jerked her closer to him, stirring a need in her that was as frightening as it was taboo. 'Because you won't let it?' As he dipped his head she could feel the heat of his breath against her throat, found herself aching for the touch of his lips...

'No, you mustn't!' With a fear that gave her strength she struggled until he released her. 'We can't! I—'

'Can't?' His laugh was coldly cynical.

'You don't understand.' Despair underlaid the panic in the eyes she lifted to his. 'We were wrong, Blaine. Your father told me. He had an affair with my mother.'

Red streaked across his hair from the wall-lights as he shook his head. 'So what's that got to do with us?'

Dear heaven! Why couldn't he understand?

She took a deep breath. 'We had no right to fall in love! Can't you see what I'm trying to say?' Her eyes were desperately searching his in a torturous appeal to him not to make her spell it out. And then softly—tremulously—she said, 'I'm your sister, Blaine.'

If he had looked gaunt before, now the bones of his cheeks stood out in proud relief and his skin appeared bloodless beneath his tan.

'What the hell are you saying?' He looked as though he had been punched. Which he had, Lydia thought. Emotionally, anyway.

'It's true,' she whispered. 'He didn't want to tell me at first. He hoped he could buy me off without saying anything. When he realised he couldn't, he had to tell me. My mother never told me who my father was. But your father had an affair with her during the year I was born. That makes us half-brother and sister, Blaine. That's why I couldn't marry you. He couldn't let us.'

He was still shaking his head. Still unable to believe it, she thought, understanding the numbing shock he had to be feeling, though she was thankful that at least he would be spared the utter devastation she had known.

'I suppose the money was to buy my silence. Some sort of…compensation.' She said it with derisive poignancy. 'As if anything could—' She cut her sentence short. What was the point of telling him that nothing could compensate for the agony she had suffered in knowing she could never love him in the way she had wanted to? That even losing him in death would have been easier because at least then she wouldn't have had to stop loving him? 'I suppose he wanted to try and keep me quiet because he couldn't face you or your mother finding out I was his daughter. Perhaps he—'

A sound from across the room brought their attention jointly to the fact that the door was now half open, and to the tall, robed figure standing there, listening in silence.

'Mother!'

'Judith!'

They spoke in unison, although it was Blaine who recovered enough self-possession, in spite of everything, to carry on.

'How long have you been there?'

Judith came in, and said quietly, 'Long enough.'

'Then you heard?' It was Blaine, looking drawn and yet still surprisingly controlled, despite the shock he had suffered.

'Yes.'

'Everything?'

'Enough,' said his mother. In her dark blue silk robe she looked pale, Lydia thought. Her eyes were heavy, purplish underneath from grief and immense fatigue.

'Did you know about this?' Blaine continued to interrogate while Lydia could only listen, feeling for Judith, weighing her own emotions against the tremendous jolt the woman had just received.

'I knew he had affairs.' She came towards them, her hands hanging limply at her sides. And even while Lydia was silently sympathising, suddenly Judith was rounding on her. 'Now perhaps you don't need a reason for my wanting you to go home!'

Lydia guessed it was because the woman was upset that she seemed to want to vent her frustrations upon her. Understandingly, therefore, she uttered, 'I'm sorry, Judith. I didn't mean for you to find out like that. For you to find out at all.'

'So you know now, Blaine.' Judith sounded resigned, weary, breathless almost, yet something about that statement made Lydia wonder if, in fact, the woman herself had known.

'Yes.' Perhaps Blaine hadn't detected it, she thought, catching his heavily exhaled response. He was probably still too stunned to fully comprehend anything, despite the self-possessed way in which he had been speaking to his mother a moment ago. 'And all these years I've been thinking the worst about her.' His gaze rested solely on Lydia now. 'Despising you...' The intensity of emotion in his voice, in those eyes, made her want to run to him, put her arms around him and feel the comfort of his, but that was out of the question. 'Why didn't you tell me?' The words escaped him on a shuddering breath.

'I couldn't. I was afraid.' Of what we'd meant to each other. Of the way we'd been.

She didn't say it. She didn't need to. He read it in her eyes—in the trembling of her voice—and understood. She could tell that just by looking at him.

For a moment there was a sensual pull so great between them she thought she would faint with the effort to struggle against it, and guessed that Judith sensed it too, when the woman said with a quiet, tight-lipped determination, 'She'll have to leave.'

Lydia pressed her lids closed against the woman's obvious lack of forgiveness for Lydia simply being her husband's illegitimate daughter, for something that wasn't her fault. When she opened them again it was to see Blaine watching her, his grey eyes burning with something dark, almost possessive.

'If she's my half-sister, she's every right to be here.' he stated, with an inflexion undermining the hard resolve of his statement. 'Wherever I go—she's a right to be.'

So he would acknowledge her. Accept her into his family as his father had never done. Dear God! She couldn't bear it! She couldn't!

Then she was aware of Judith—like an insulator between two conductive elements—saying, 'But it isn't that simple, is it, Blaine?'

His face seemed to grow rigid, and his chest lifted and fell with one laboured, shuddering breath.

'Oh, God!' he whispered, massaging the tight muscles at the base of his neck.

Anger and frustration rippled through every inch of him, and then he turned and strode out, leaving Lydia and Judith facing each other in silence.

'You knew, didn't you?' Lydia remarked, hearing the

outer door slam closed behind Blaine. She was convinced of it now. 'You knew all about it.' And, when the woman didn't answer, 'If you knew, why didn't you tell him?' she uttered with accusing poignancy.

She watched Judith take a breath, stalling for time. She seemed to be weighing her words very carefully.

'There didn't seem any point in discrediting his father unnecessarily. You were out of his life. I didn't think it would do anyone any good dragging up the past.'

'But to let him go on—believing the worst possible things he could believe about me...' She choked on her words, her expression a mixture of disbelief and pained perplexity. 'Didn't you care how it might have affected me?'

The sob in her voice was drowned by the deep sound of the clock striking in the hall. One. Two. Two o'clock, and then the sudden growl of the Mercedes—like a small explosion in the still of the night—as it started up on the drive.

'Lydia...' Tentatively, Judith raised her hand to Lydia's shoulder, but let it fall again before it had actually made contact. 'I didn't...' She shook her head, as though in negation of whatever she had been about to say. 'As I said just now, you were out of his life.'

'I was never out of his life,' Lydia responded, sadly aware of it now. And, sensing that there was nothing more to say or to be said, she left Judith and made her way back upstairs.

So Blaine had gone out—unable to cope with the truth that she had hit him with. But where? Would he just drive around the island? Or would he, in need of a consolation he couldn't trust himself to find with her, seek solace in Shelley Graham's arms?

Hot emotion, as intense as any jealousy could be, reared its ugly head, astounding her with her capacity to feel so cheated.

He's your half-brother! she reminded herself, with a fierceness that reflected the scale of her emotions. And, giving in to them now, she flung herself down onto her rumpled bed, her control finally broken, torn from her in convulsive sobs that shook her slender body with a violence she thought she would never survive.

It rained during what was left of the night, a torrential downpour that tore through the tall palms surrounding the property like an army of angry feet.

When she awoke—because, amazingly, she had slept—and heavily—she thought, from the pattering through the palms, that it was still raining. A peep through the venetian blind, however, revealed that it was only the wind playing with the crisp, feather-shaped leaves, and that in actuality it was a beautiful day.

The sun was shining gold across the pool terrace, bouncing colours off the crystal water, visible from the window, as she came down into the airy breakfast room where Judith was sitting alone, finishing a light breakfast.

'Good morning,' she said formally, folding her copy of the *Royal Gazette* on top of her carefully folded napkin. Even in conflict, Lydia thought, Judith wouldn't allow good breeding and protocol to desert her.

Lydia merely nodded in response. 'Have you seen Liam?' she enquired anxiously. He hadn't been in his room when she had looked in there a moment ago.

'He's on the verandah. It's Blaine I'm more worried about,' Judith expressed, turning on her chair. In her rather formal skirt and blouse she made Lydia feel almost bohemian in her sparse broderie-anglaise camisole that picked out the yellow in her own diaphanous, multi-coloured skirt. 'He hasn't come home.'

Unconsciously, Lydia bit her lip, her gaze moving automatically to the door. 'I'm sure he's all right.'

'Are you?' Judith's query was almost angry. The circles under her eyes appeared darker this morning, Lydia noticed, and thought the woman looked as distressed as she did, if that were possible. 'What makes you so sure, Lydia? After all he's been through…' Lydia didn't need to be told that Judith meant the traumas surrounding her daughter-in-law and her grandson. 'Oh! Why did you have to come here? Why couldn't you leave things as they were?'

With Blaine hating her and Liam believing his father despised him, as it was obvious he did?

'And not told him?' Lydia challenged, so that a hue spread upwards across the fine, pale skin of her cheeks. 'I had to.'

'Oh, yes, I realise that!' It came out on a despairing little laugh. 'My son's far too smitten with you to have made it possible for you not to tell him. Why don't you do the right thing now and go home—and leave us all in peace?'

Imperceptibly Lydia flinched, rubbing her arms as though they were suddenly cold.

Peace. Hardly that, she thought, considering the emotions that continued to ravage his household.

'I know you don't like me, Judith,' she uttered with genuine regret. How could she be expected to when she, Lydia, had been conceived through Henry Caldwell's affair with another woman? 'But can't we try to be friends for everyone's sake? As soon as Blaine wants me to go—I'll go.' Or as soon as Heather can come up with a replacement, she thought, adding aloud, 'I don't want to stay here any longer than is absolutely necessary.'

Judith didn't answer, her expression troubled as she glanced down at the fine used crockery on the table.

Well, you couldn't force anyone to feel what they didn't want to feel, Lydia thought with a little shrug, today able to resist the plate of freshly baked croissants the kitchen had sent in, wandering out instead to find Liam.

The breeze made ripples on the pool as she took the long way round across the terrace. A speedboat hummed way off in the golden waters of the harbour and two kiskadees squabbled on top of one of the white chimneys above the house.

The wind strewed some frangipani blossoms across the verandah as she came up onto it, looking for Liam, their scent evocative and heady. The boy, though, was nowhere to be seen.

He hadn't gone inside. Some deep and primal intuition told her that. Worriedly she raced back down the steps, past the hibiscus hedges to the beach, but the pale warm crescent of sand was deserted, save for a gull foraging on the waterline, which took off with a shriek of indignation as soon as it saw her.

She ran up from the beach and along the jetty, knowing it was useless wondering even before she looked across to the two sleek craft innocently moored there in the sunlight. He would never have attempted anything so dangerous unaided.

And then she heard it, a sound that made her look up

to the unfenced piece of land at the far end of the cove, above the jagged symmetry of the rocks.

'*Liam.*' She dared not raise her voice above a whisper, as though to do so would make him tumble and fall from the precarious position in which he was standing near the very edge of the rocks. 'Liam!' This time she yelled at the top of her voice. He stopped. He had heard her. She breathed a deep sigh of relief. 'Stay where you are! I'm coming up!'

She was already running back up through the lush vegetation to the stretch of lawn that separated the house from the volcanic cliffs. The grass was still wet underfoot, which meant that the rocks would be slippery and dangerous too, from the far too recent shower.

She didn't know what happened next, only that one moment he was standing there, a small dark figure against the backdrop of the ocean, and then the next his feet seemed to slide from under him.

'Liam!' She screamed, but it was useless, and helplessly she watched as his cane clattered onto the hard ground and then disappeared with its little owner over the edge.

CHAPTER SEVEN

LYDIA'S breath came in painful gasps when she reached the spot where she had seen Liam fall. Gingerly, she moved to the edge and peered over.

Mercifully, he hadn't fallen in the water! Or was it mercifully? she thought, because he was lying in an awkward position, face down, on a wide shelf of rock a couple of metres below her.

'Liam!' The boy remained motionless, despite her urgent call, and Lydia's hand flew to her mouth, her eyes dark with a sickening fear.

What if he was badly injured? What if…?

She forced herself to breathe deeply to get some grip on her runaway emotions. She didn't want to think about that.

Her feet threatened to give way on the uneven rocks as she sought desperately to find a way down to him.

Don't let him be badly hurt, she prayed silently, realising almost immediately that it was impossible to negotiate any safe route down, or even to try and rescue him herself. Even though the cliff was reasonably shallow, it provided no easy access to him from here. She would have to get help.

'Don't worry, Liam! I'll get help!' she called again, hoping that he could hear and understand. 'I won't be long.'

She had to find Blaine. It was her only thought as she

tore back across the grass, her skirt catching round her legs, threatening to trip her.

But Blaine wasn't there, was he? He had gone out last night and hadn't come back this morning. There was Simon, but he was a middle-aged man and less than agile. And Judith wouldn't be able to do any more than Lydia could herself. She wanted to weep with fear and frustration. So what was she supposed to do? Call an ambulance? Call the coastguard? Or some other rescue service? What if they weren't in time? What if…?

Her mind a whirl of chaotic thoughts, she raced along the path in front of the house, past the frangipani tree and up the verandah steps, glancing back briefly when she reached the top, only to let out a small cry as she collided with something substantial and warm.

'Blaine!' She could scarcely breathe his name she was panting so hard. Her lungs felt as if they were on fire.

'What is it? Lydia, what is it?' Concern etched deep lines into his face, a countenance harshened by the incredibly dark shadow around his jaw. His hair was dishevelled, windblown. 'What's wrong?' Urgently his gaze ran over her flushed and stricken features, and his fingers bit into her flesh where he was having to virtually shake her to get her to make some sense.

'It's Liam!' Never had she been so glad to see anyone in her life. Hastily, between tearful gasps, she enlightened him as to what had happened. She could give in to her frustration now because he was here. He would take control. 'He was out on the verandah, Judith said. I didn't know he was going to wander off like that. Oh, Blaine! I didn't know!'

'Never mind that now!' She could feel the tightening of muscle beneath the shirt he was still wearing from the previous night, the shock and revelations of hours before temporarily shelved because of this new and more pressing situation as he put her from him and started swiftly down the steps.

'No, not that way!' he called as she made to dart back towards the cliff-edge. 'We'll just be wasting valuable time by going that way!'

Of course he would know, she thought, wishing she had his speed and stamina as she ran after him down through the shrubbery.

He headed straight for the jetty, and, when she caught up, pulled her after him into the bobbing hulk of the launch.

'What are you going to do?' she panted between breaths.

'See if I can get to him from below rather than above,' he answered above the sudden noisy burring of the engine. 'For heaven's sake, sit down!' he ordered then, because she was rocking the boat and putting them both at risk.

Not needing to be told twice, she obeyed.

They were already speeding away from the narrow wall of the jetty, and Lydia's heart was in her mouth as they came around the jagged elevation of the rocks.

Would Liam be conscious? Alive, even? He hadn't fallen that far, but depending upon how awkwardly or hard he had struck the ground it could mean the difference between slight or serious—or even fatal—injury.

Her heart-rate had scarcely slackened, fear and only fear keeping it racing now as Blaine brought the launch close to the dark promontory of the rocks.

She could see, though, why he had decided on making the rescue attempt from here instead of by the almost impossible route down from the top. Here the rocks were stepped part of the way up, enabling one to effect a surer, though still somewhat risky climb, and some scrub, growing just overhead, offered an advantage, Lydia realised, as Blaine utilised one of the stunted trees as a makeshift mooring for the launch.

'You stay here,' he commanded as those strong hands gave a hard jerk, securing the rope.

'No,' she defied, getting up just as he was about to step out. After all, he was going to need all the help he could get. 'I'm coming with you, so don't try and stop me.'

For a moment, with those broad shoulders squaring, he looked as though he was going to. But perhaps he thought this wasn't the time for arguing, she decided, when all he said in surprising acquiescence was, 'Then keep close to me.'

The boat bobbed and dipped as he stepped lithely onto the rocks, then turned to assist Lydia out of the boat.

His hand was warm and firm as it clasped hers. Their eyes met and held and Lydia felt an exchange of something raw and poignant pass between them which neither dared voice or acknowledge as he pulled her up safely beside him.

'Be careful,' he advised, and his voice was thick with an emotion as stretched as the tension inside herself.

It was an easier climb than she'd imagined to where Liam was lying.

Fast-moving clouds sailed above them on the rocky shelf, fluffy white against the azure sky. Briefly Lydia glimpsed the immaculate roof and white chimneys of the house, and the swaying palms to the right of it that marked the boundary with its neighbour, before she dropped swiftly down beside Blaine to attend to Liam.

'My goodness, Blaine. Is he going to be all right?' Looking at the prostrate young figure in shorts and T-shirt, she didn't think he'd moved at all, and she knew a dread as dark as doom when he didn't respond to Blaine's gentle shaking of his shoulder.

With a weakening queasiness in her stomach, she watched him ease Liam round to face him and apply urgent but gentle fingers to the boy's throat.

'Well, his pulse is strong enough.' Above the wash of the sea over the rocks below, there was a choking relief in his voice now, a relief which Lydia felt and which had her sinking to her knees beside him.

'Thank goodness! Oh, thank goodness!'

And then, through a blur of grateful tears, suddenly she saw Liam move. He groaned and then opened his eyes, turned his head in that distinctive way he had whenever he grasped a sound, and on a note of painful query that was reflected in his face he uttered, 'Dad?'

'Liam.'

As he struggled to sit up, suddenly Blaine was clasping his son fiercely to him.

'Dear God,' he whispered, his words trembling with the shudders that seemed to be racking that strong body. 'I don't know what I would have done if I'd lost you, too.'

Behind him, she saw Liam's arms come automatically to his father's shoulders, automatically but hesitantly, as though he were uncertain of how to respond to his father's very real emotion. And the next moment they were entwining almost as fiercely around Blaine's neck.

Witnessing the bridging of a gulf that had seemed

unbridgeable before, Lydia felt her heart go out to Blaine—to both of them.

'Are you in any pain? Where does it hurt?' she heard him gently asking Liam.

And the boy's rather anguished response, 'It's just my leg...'

Deftly, Blaine probed the area Liam had indicated with the same tentative gentleness that made Lydia's throat ache with a suffocating emotion. There was a nasty graze on the thin, grubby knee.

'And a bump on the head, son,' Blaine told him softly, that wry twist to his mouth displaying his deep affection for the twelve-year-old which until now had been tenaciously repressed. 'I think your leg's going to be fine, but it's the bump I think we'd better get checked out, don't you?' His smile hid the anxiety, apparent to Lydia, in his voice. 'Can you stand up?'

He could, but only painfully, and without further delay Blaine lifted him up into his arms.

Getting to her feet, anxiously Lydia put out an ineffectual arm. 'Can you manage?' she queried, feeling totally useless, unable to do anything but retrieve the cane that had been lying nearby. Blaine might be stronger than a lot of men, but one slip of the foot...

'Yes. Just watch where you're going,' he advised in a firm voice. 'I don't want two stretcher cases on my hands.'

With no mention of last night, she thought, as she started the rocky descent ahead of him. But then he had had too much to think about since he had come back. Momentarily, then, she wondered where he had spent the previous night, and decided that if it was with Shelley Graham she didn't want to know.

Though not very far, it was nevertheless a hazardous climb down to the launch. Just below her the boat dipped and rose on a sea made choppy by a rising wind.

Gingerly, Lydia stepped down onto the lower rocks, leaning forward to grasp the side of the craft so that she could pull it hard against them. Her arm hurt after a while, from trying to hold it steady, but at least she managed to do so, stifling her discomfort as Blaine trod carefully down onto the wet volcanic surface beside her and lowered his son gently into the boat.

'Go on. I've got it,' he said imperatively, steadying the launch himself so that she could step aboard, for which she was immensely grateful. Her arm felt as though it had been pulled out of its socket.

Sitting with her arm around Liam, whose head was resting against her shoulder, she felt the launch dip as Blaine stepped aboard, the displacement of the water lapping around them.

Unable to help herself, she watched him unfasten the rope tied around the scrub, noticing with reluctant fascination the play of muscle beneath his shirt as those capable hands worked, pulling in the line.

Suddenly he turned round, before she could look away, and his expression was one of such unimagined bleakness that it was like a blow, temporarily striking the breath out of her lungs.

What was he thinking? she wondered achingly, her gaze holding his for a long moment while she tried to fathom something—anything—from the unfathomable, because his face was a rigid mask now, revealing nothing.

'Let's get him back,' was all he said curtly, turning away.

*   *   *

Fortunately, Liam's injuries were not serious. His leg and hip were only bruised, they were told, after Lydia had insisted on accompanying him and Blaine to the hospital, but they were advised that as the boy had been concussed it was best to keep him in overnight for observation.

'It's only routine,' the buxom Bermudian sister told them with a smile before they went back into the little side-ward where Liam had been taken.

Despite his fall, he looked well enough, Lydia considered, seeing him tucked up in bed, fiddling with the controls of the radio that one of the nurses must have helped him to locate.

'Why did you wander off like that, Liam?' Blaine asked him after a while, now he was assured his son was going to be all right. But he wasn't angry, just concerned, and the boy answered without any rebellion, responding to that caring note in his father's voice.

'I heard Lydia arguing with Gran, and Gran said she had to go away. I don't want her to go away. I want her to stay.'

Lydia caught her breath as that familiar ache, dislodged by the day's events, returned with crushing intensity to her chest.

Across the bed she met Blaine's gaze, felt its power like the tug of a dangerous undercurrent, its pull as frightening, threatening to swamp any resistance she might attempt.

'Don't we both want her to stay, son?'

Though her eyes didn't leave his, she was aware of that long bronzed hand closing over the smaller one of Liam's that was lying on the white sheet, and a surge of anger welled up inside of her, anger mingling with un-speakable pain, turning her sapphire eyes almost to jet.

She shook her head, the movement barely discernible.

How could he? How could he tell Liam that when he knew it was impossible? That it would be torture for her—if not for him—every minute that she stayed!

He got up then, squeezing Liam's hand. 'Gran's get-ting Simon to bring her over to see you later,' he said, having phoned Judith earlier to let her know her grand-son was all right. 'Then, hopefully, tomorrow you'll be able to come home.'

Liam's head inclined as he looked in the general di-rection of his father. 'But you're going away, aren't you? I heard you telling Simon yesterday—you're going back to New York.'

Lydia looked at Blaine quickly. She, too, was on her feet.

Of course. He had business to attend to, which was why she had been engaged in the first place, she remem-bered, noticing the tightening of that strong, unshaven jaw before he finally responded.

'No, Liam. I'm not going away,' he said decisively.

'Promise,' the boy uttered, with very Blaine-like per-sistence.

'Promise,' he whispered softly, placing a kiss—with-out any sign of embarrassment or awkwardness—ten-derly on the boy's forehead. 'Now get some rest, little warrior.'

Lydia kissed him too, her voice cracking as she spoke. 'Bye, Liam.'

Perhaps they would heal, she thought. The wounds between father and son. Oh, not as quickly as Liam's physical injuries, perhaps, but just as surely, she re-

flected as she went ahead of Blaine along the clean,
scrubbed corridor. But as she stepped out into the blaz-
ing Bermuda afternoon, she doubted that she would see
a day when her own emotional wounds—opened up
again by coming here—would ever heal.

The roads were awash with colour as they started their
scenic journey back to the house. Hibiscus, growing as
profusely as weeds, filled the hedgerows with their flam-
boyant beauty, while the pinks and reds of oleander
made a fragrant canopy above the car along some of the
narrower lanes.

Travelling along at the leisurely speed limit, Blaine
lifted one hand to the back of his neck. The lines around
his eyes were emphasised today, making him look
tired—extremely weary—and Lydia told him as much.

'Yes.' He exhaled heavily, bringing his hand back
onto the steering wheel. 'You could say that.'

Well, it was no more than expected, she thought.
What with all that had transpired with Liam coming immediately after his discovery that she was his half-
sister...

She needed to talk to him—to have him talk to her—
and after a while, because he was just sitting there, steering the car and looking grim, she took a deep breath and
said, 'You didn't come back last night.'

'No.'

But with no explanation as to where he had been—or
with whom.

Strung with tension, she gazed out of the window,
staring sightlessly at the white-roofed millionaire mansions, at the blue sea, glimpsed between pastel cottages,

at the flaming red of a poinciana tree in one front garden, sporting its blossoms like a fiery crest.

She wasn't aware of Blaine's brief glances in her direction, the way his gaze fell, for as long as it was safe to do so, on the taut beauty of her features.

'Why didn't you tell me?' he asked suddenly then, his voice soft over the gentle purr of the Mercedes.

His dark gaze caught hers now, causing her heart to give a swift lurch before he directed his attention to the road again.

'Why did you pretend to be having an affair with Tyndall? Just to get rid of me?' he asked incredulously. 'Why? Why couldn't you have told me the truth? Instead of letting me believe—'

Something close to frustration harshened his voice, bringing him up short as he pulled out rather sharply to avoid a cyclist. He was in no shape to be holding a conversation like this and still have control of the car.

'Do you want me to drive?' she offered tentatively when he had pulled back onto the right side of the white line. He had to be exhausted at the very least.

'Why? Don't you think I'm capable?' Now she glimpsed a wry, self-denigrating smile pull at that rigid mouth.

'No, but...'

'Answer my question, Lydia.'

She chewed on her upper lip and glanced away from him, out of her window again.

They were passing a shopping mart, very American in design. People emerged, clutching the proverbial brown paper bag she was used to seeing in American films and television soaps. Despite being British,

Bermuda was heavily influenced by its closest and most powerful neighbour, she thought, turning away.

'I told you last night. I was frightened. Of your father. Of myself,' she admitted, with a rather pained glance in his direction. 'And your father said he could end my career if I dared let it out about his affair with my mother.'

'My father said *that?*' His tone was sceptical, as though he were having some difficulty accepting it as he looked down at the slim hand picking absently at the bright gauzy fabric of her skirt. 'So you kept quiet about it,' he said thickly, 'for the sake of your career.'

Was that what it had sounded like?

There was a stark denial in her face as her head came up now. 'No. By then, after he told me why I couldn't marry you, I didn't give a damn about my career. When he offered me the chance to fake an affair with Jeremy I grabbed it, even though I knew it was going to half kill me to carry it through. I was young and scared, and your father said he wouldn't have any scandal. It was my reputation on the line to protect everyone else's.'

'Is that what he advised you?' His tone was scathing.

'Well, he had a family to think about.' She tried to sound understanding—reasonable. But the fact that she was Henry Caldwell's daughter—albeit unwanted by him—and he could still throw her on the mercy of the press as he had was something that still cut her to the core. Often she had suspected that his attempted pay-off had been offered solely to salve his own conscience, but she didn't tell Blaine that, going on in a voice nevertheless coloured with bitterness, 'He was a prominent businessman and I was just the model everyone wanted to read about—thanks to the legacy of a rather infamous actress for a mother! The people who buy those sorts of newspapers expected—probably wanted—to see me following in her footsteps.'

'And you didn't let them down.'

As he negotiated a busy junction, Blaine's incisive reminder of those months following their break-up when she had tried to submerge her misery in a sea of publicity made her inwardly recoil.

'I was trying to forget you. That's why I kept myself so busy.'

'Busy?' There was a jagged edge to his voice as he levelled the car along the road that would take them out to the eastern fringes of the island. 'Dating a different man every week?'

'Yes, *dating*,' she emphasised, to try and make him realise that there had never been anything more to those platonic relationships that the papers had reported on with such gusto. 'Sometimes. More often they were just colleagues I worked with. Promotions men. Actors. Photographers. I just had to have lunch with someone between shoots and I was conducting a full-blown love affair! None of them meant anything to me. I was lonely and devastated and—'

'Yes?' he prompted when she failed to finish. But she couldn't, sitting there with her face turned away from his so that he didn't notice the anguish graven on her youthful features, any more than she noticed the sun glittering on blue water, or the small craft moored in a quiet marina on her side of the car.

This man wasn't the prospective lover she had once imagined she'd be spending her life with. The blood-ties between them were too close for her to be telling him these things—like her innermost secrets and the turmoil that had driven her to perfect her act of mock indifference to what everyone had been saying about her, like her feelings for him.

'But you didn't come and tell me the truth,' he persisted, fortunately not pressing her to continue with whatever she had been about to say. 'Why you were breaking off our engagement.'

'I couldn't bear it,' was all she could utter in a whisper.

'So you preferred to make me hate you.' His statement was unrelenting, deeply critical.

It wasn't until he swung the Mercedes across the road, indicating right, that she noticed the lay-by he was pulling into, overlooking the ocean.

The click of the handbrake spelled a harrowing intimacy, heightened by the screaming silence that followed.

'I wanted to tell you,' she confided then, torn by the animosity and resentment he must have harboured towards her—and until as recently as yesterday. 'For a time afterwards I kept telling myself that when I had come to terms with it, no matter what your father wanted, I probably would tell you—eventually. I spent weeks wrestling with what would be the right thing to do.'

'And "the right thing to do" was to let me go on in the dark. Wondering. Despising you...'

'No.' She felt his hard, questioning glance but couldn't look at him, keeping her attention instead on the smooth grey leather of the dashboard.

He had changed earlier, but had had no chance to shower or shave in his haste to get Liam to the hospital. Her nostrils, therefore, were too alert to the stirring traces of perspiration on his skin, the dark stubble around his jaw making him remind her of some marauding Spanish buccaneer, who might once have sailed into these islands, negotiating his ship and crew through the treacherous reef.

'No,' she said again, in answer to his remark about the right thing being not to tell him, although neither could she confess to exactly what it was that had stopped her. Never—*never*—would she ever tell him that.

But she had to say something, and, with her lashes concealing her eyes and the dark emotion they contained, she murmured, 'You married Sharon. And then everything seemed pointless.'

Against the rumble of a truck passing on the other side of the road, she caught his swift inhalation, and jumped as he struck the steering wheel with a vehement fist.

'Well, as you said—' he exhaled with something corrosive in those deep, rich tones '—then everything seemed pointless.'

Had it? Lydia darted a glance at the hard curve of his cheek, at the unyielding line of his mouth, induced by some memory she couldn't begin to guess at. Had his marriage been a failure—as he'd admitted to it being last night—right from the beginning?

Her gaze slid down his left arm to where it rested on the wheel. The bronze flesh was feathered with silky hair. The muscles beneath the sinewy limb were bunched with the same tension that harshened the angles of his profile. And though he was leaning forward, so that she couldn't see his expression, she could sense the desolation in those grey eyes staring sightlessly at the light traffic coming towards them on the stretch of tarmac, fringed on his side by the restless sea.

An aching emotion swept so forcefully through Lydia that she made a move towards him, wanting to place her hand on his arm, lay her head against the curve of his broad back, finding the need so great that she had to clench her fists and hold her body rigid to stop herself from doing so. This wasn't familial affection she felt for him. This was something darker, something she had to renounce, or go mad under the strength of her own sickening responses to it.

'So that's it, then. Lydia Lawrence. My half-sister!' The rancour in his laugh provoked an icy shudder down her spine. 'My father really loused it up, didn't he? Why, of all the women I had to meet, did I have to pick on his bastard offspring?' The soft leather beneath him squeaked as he leaned back, looking at her as though it was all her fault. His expression was disdainful, almost condemning. 'So what am I supposed to do? Simply accept you as my little sister? Just like that? When I still—'

Still what? Still wanted her? Was that what he had been going to say?

His hand on the back of her seat, close to her shoulder beneath the pale lemon top, made her shrink away, alarm flaring in her eyes. She didn't think she could cope with even the barest contact with him. Cope with these feelings that were totally taboo!

'Oh, don't worry. I'm not going to touch you,' he rasped, his mouth twisting as though in hard derision of any such concept. 'As you said, it's so bloody lucky nothing happened! Thanks to your mother—and your staunch determination never to be like her—we were never lovers—not in the true sense anyway! Isn't that what you want me to shout from the rooftops, Lydia? My father's timing couldn't have been more impeccable, could it? Who knows what might have transpired if he hadn't sent me away?'

His tone was cruel and sarcastic, challenging her to deny the celibacy she had forced upon them during their brief betrothal; challenging her to forget his frustration, and yet his gentle understanding too.

But of course he had said it himself. *They had never been lovers!* Never! Only ever in her dreams.

Without her being wholly aware of it, she realised that Blaine had started the car, and as he pulled away, crossing the lane of on-coming traffic, absently she looked down at her hands.

They were still clenched into tight fists, so tight it was causing her actual physical pain. Her knuckles were white, her fingers stiff, and when she uncurled them she was shocked to see the red indentations in the centre of each palm, and the small pin-pricks of blood where her nails had cut into the soft flesh.

Liam was allowed home the following day. Blaine and Judith went to fetch him, while Lydia stayed behind at the house.

She couldn't face spending much time with Blaine— with either of them—but particularly Blaine.

His attitude towards her had hardened, if anything, and it hurt, even though she realised that it sprang from shock over his discovery of who she really was, plus an inborn sense of anger and frustration in finding things, for once, totally beyond his control.

For herself, she would have liked to have gone home,

but he had made her promise to stay in Bermuda at least until Liam recovered, and out of her respect and sympathy for the boy's wishes she had agreed. It was, after all, indirectly because of her that Liam had wandered off like that, ironically because he'd been upset when he'd thought she was being sent home.

Consequently, she had telephoned Heather that morning to advise her that she would probably be staying at least another week.

'That's great!' Heather had enthused. 'Does that mean little Lyddie's grateful to her old Auntie Heather now?'

Grateful! Lydia had had to bite her tongue to keep her raging emotions in check.

'On the contrary,' she'd informed her colleague tightly, without giving any reason for her clipped response. 'And when little Lyddie gets home she's going to strangle you, Auntie Heather!'

Her partner had been eager to discover why, but Lydia hadn't felt like talking and had rung off quickly. There would be enough time to explain, she told herself now—if ever she felt inclined to—down the long, lonely years ahead.

Because she had decided once and for all that nothing could ever replace the feelings she had felt for Blaine. Feelings which, heaven help her!—though no one else would ever know it—*she* knew with a sick acknowledgement she would always feel for him. Oh, she could marry, and probably find a kind of happiness with someone else at some time in the future, she thought. Only that would be exactly what Blaine had done, and she didn't think that that would be fair to any partner she chose to go through life with—making promises to someone knowing that her feelings would never quite reach the heights and depths of emotion she had experienced the first time around.

Well, if it wasn't to be, it wasn't to be, she assured herself, though with bitter resignation, just as voices were heard in the hall.

'Lydia?'

It was that questioning note of Liam's, relying as he was on movement to indicate her presence as he felt his way into the lounge, with some obscure 'other' sense the sighted didn't possess.

'I'm over here.'

He smiled when he heard her voice, the swing of his cane quickening as he hobbled over to the marble table where she was standing.

She reached out an arm, and felt her heart wrenched out of her as those young, tentative fingers moved along it to enfold her in an affectionate hug.

Please don't do this! something inside her cried. You'll just make it harder for us both. And you're nothing to me. Because you can never *be* anything to me!

Her expression mirrored her feelings as she clasped his lean, warm body, as her eyes met Blaine's—dark with his own private demons—across the room.

But of course he knew as well as she did that no matter how far she might go, and how hard she might try to forget him, that infidelity that had made them half-brother and sister, ironically, would bind her to Liam and ultimately, therefore, to him, since she couldn't escape the fact that his and Sharon's son was her nephew.

CHAPTER EIGHT

LYDIA had been in Bermuda for nearly two weeks, by which time Liam was recovering satisfactorily from his fall.

Lydia, however, felt herself slipping downhill with each passing day. She had begun to lose her appetite and, if that were not enough, the nightmares had started again.

She had been prone to vivid dreams even as a child, but now—just like before, for a whole year after she'd broken up with Blaine—they were both hideous and absurd.

She woke unrefreshed, and the strain of being there in such close proximity to Blaine was beginning to show in her face.

Bravely, though, she concealed her emotions behind an enforced brightness for Liam. He had greater problems than she did, after all. And, with a cosmetic skill acquired from her modelling days, she managed to use her make-up in a way that kept her pallor and her fatigue cleverly hidden, so that no one suspected how she was really feeling.

Having been confined to the house for nearly a week, Liam was getting restless. As soon as he could walk, therefore, without any sign of discomfort, and with Blaine out that morning and using the car, Lydia called a cab to take them both to Hamilton.

A carriage ride around the city was the first treat, she

decided, remembering how taken Liam had been with
the horses on the quayside that day they had met Judith
off the ship. Then an ice-cream, the biggest he could
manage, was the second order of the day, before they
hopped on to one of the island's pink and blue buses to
visit the much advertised Botanical Gardens.

A thirty-six-acre estate, the gardens surrounded the
official residence of Bermuda's premier, a colonial-style
mansion flanked by exotic trees and fronted by a profusion of flowers that made a bright hem around an immaculately kept lawn. The park also laid claim to wide
areas of open space, an aviary, specialised flower gardens and, to Lydia's surprise and delight, a garden for
the blind.

'They knew we were coming, Liam,' she laughed
when they came upon the small walled area.

Seriously, to herself, though, she thought what partic-
ular care had been taken in its design, because the
flowers were mainly distinctive to the touch and highly
perfumed, to help anyone with visual difficulties in iden-
tifying them. A fountain added a serenity of sound to
catch the ear, and the crunchy surface underfoot meant
that Liam had no problem staying within the boundaries
of the path.

Surprisingly, visiting the aviary afterwards delighted
Liam as much as anything else, and they laughed together at one exotic bird which kept flying down to
perch on the wire, level with Liam, so that it could nib-
ble gently at his finger through the cage.

It was good to see him laughing after all the problems
he had had to deal with, Lydia thought when they
stepped out into the sunshine again. And since that open
display of affection by his father after his fall the pre-

vious week, the change in Liam had been gradual, though apparent, and things were becoming easier now between him and Blaine.

There was only one low moment, when they were taking a leisurely stroll through an open area of the park and two children raced out from behind a bank of ornamental trees, a boy and a girl, so engrossed in their game of tag that they nearly collided with Liam. Flushed-faced, they made swift and unembarrassed apologies.

'I wish I had a brother,' he commented, envious of their shared laughter and the argument that was ensuing over whose turn it was to give chase as they darted away. 'If you stayed here and married Dad, I could have some brothers and sisters.'

The warm wind soughing through the bright blossoms of an unfamiliar shrub, contrarily, seemed to chill her. Emotions ran riot through her, robbing her of any immediate response.

And then a deep voice, threaded with tension, instantly recognisable, cut across the silence.

'Liam!' It was a touch of the old austerity, immediately tempered by a rather strained smile as Blaine strode over to them, still dressed for business in a short-sleeved white shirt and tie and very lightweight suit trousers. 'You presume too much, young man.' A strong hand ruffled the boy's dark hair, its touch repentant, reassuring.

'Blaine!' What was he doing there? How had he managed to materialise as though from thin air?

'I saw you hop on that bus in Hamilton,' he explained wryly, seeing the puzzled question in her eyes. 'I was tied up with a client so I couldn't just rush away. I asked

Simon if he knew if you'd be likely to be coming here.'
And Simon had told him, she thought with a knowing
smile, remembering she'd asked the chauffeur about
these gardens only the previous morning. 'I just hoped
you'd still be here.'

Lydia's smile broadened. 'So here we are,' she said
with a casual gesture of her arms, and felt his gaze touch
cursorily on her gentle curves beneath her white V-
necked top and yellow shorts.

'Liam, why don't you take this and see if it's to your
satisfaction?' Blaine suggested, pulling something from
the pocket of his trousers.

'My Walkman!' the boy recognised, beaming when
his father took one young hand in his and placed the
small black square onto its palm.

'Complete with earphones.' Blaine's regard was
touching, Lydia thought, with something catching at her
heart from the familiar tilt of his dark head as he plugged
the little black wire into the relevant socket. He had
taken the Walkman to be repaired a couple of days ago,
she remembered, recalling how much Liam had missed
having it. 'And it was the number-one-selling album
you've been dying to get your hands on, wasn't it?'

'You bought it!' Liam's face was a picture as, with
an arm around his shoulders, Blaine guided him towards
a convenient wooden seat, secluded beneath the riotous
colour of a large oleander bush.

'You've really made his day,' Lydia commented,
smiling indulgently towards the happy adolescent sitting
there in his element, head moving rhythmically to some
undetectable music. 'You're doing great, Blaine.'

'Am I?' He sounded sceptical.

'Of course.' Her smile wavered as she looked at him.

Mature, self-contained, and with that raw masculine confidence which in the past she had found formidably daunting, he nevertheless possessed a vulnerability that called to an aching void deep down inside of her. 'All you have to do is go on as you're going and you'll have a wonderful future together. You're still the best thing he's ever likely to have.'

There was an affectionate twist to her mouth as she studied the boy's happy countenance.

His music was everything to him, she thought, pushing back a windblown strand of dark hair behind her ear, exposing the high curve of her forehead, the exquisite contouring of her cheek and jaw.

'And you're still the most beautiful woman I've ever known.'

Her heart seemed to stop beating, so that everything around them, from the lavish landscaping to a group of people from a wedding party she had noticed earlier in the formal garden, who were now standing, talking, some distance away, seemed locked inside a frozen tableau.

'I suppose a man can still say that about his sister.' He had become harder and more cynical since the day after he had found out—if not with her or with Liam, then more generally at any rate.

'Blaine, please...'

He laughed tightly, his head coming up, revealing the dark, corded strength of his throat. 'Why? Aren't you able to handle compliments from your brother?' His description of himself came out on a positive sneer.

But that was the truth of it, she thought achingly as she watched him stoop to pick up a sad, solitary rose that was lying on the grass. She couldn't. Not from the

man she had loved enough to want to marry. The one
man she knew she never could.

'They'll think I picked it,' she said wretchedly when
he handed her the flower, although she took it anyway.
Its petals were creamy, perfect, their fragrance still lingering. Someone must have taken it from the garden near
the premier's house, then discarded it, she thought, as
though its transient beauty wasn't brief enough.

'Then let them.' The lines of his mouth were set in a
bitter cast. 'Not everything we pick in this life is out-
lawed or forbidden.'

As their love was?

Pain showed itself as a faint line between her brows
and she stared sightlessly at the rose, unable to look at
him, then gave a little gasp as he jerked her chin up
between his thumb and forefinger, holding her exposed
to those cruelly perceptive eyes.

'You look tired, Lydia.' Mercilessly his gaze raked
over the tight symmetry of her face, noticing without too
much difficulty the fine blue skin beneath her lower
lashes, the unusual pallor of her complexion that even
her clever use of make-up couldn't altogether conceal
from him.

'It's a bundle of laughs, isn't it?' he said. 'Finding
relatives one didn't know one had?' His sarcasm was
turned in on himself. Biting. Granite-hard. 'I keep looking for family resemblances.' Ignoring her small groan
of despair, roughly he tilted her chin this way and that,
studying her with a guarded inspection. 'Where do you
think they lie, Lydia? In our ability to hurt each other?
Or is it in our kindred passion for the impossible?'

'Blaine, don't!'

She pulled out of his grasp, her blood seeming to flow like a congealing river through her veins.

Sweet heaven! She couldn't bear this! She couldn't bear it!

Her gaze strayed to Liam, sitting there, happily oblivious to them, beneath the oleander bush, and absently her ears tuned to the tinny resonance from the high level of volume he had selected, drifting over to her like the faint sound of distant pipes.

'Don't you think one of us should tell him? About me, I mean,' she suggested tremulously, and looked down at the flower she had forgotten she was holding. Already its delicate petals were bruised and curling, turning brown at the edges. 'Don't you think he ought to be told that I'm his aunt?'

Someone, she had hoped, would have done it by now. But Judith seemed uncomfortable with the subject, veering away from it whenever it was broached, causing Lydia to wonder if it was because the woman simply didn't want to acknowledge her husband's illegitimate offspring as part of the family.

Now, though, Blaine's reply was just as dismissive as he plunged his hands deep into his trouser pockets and rasped, 'And what do you imagine would be gained from that?'

A child shrieked spiritedly on the other side of the park—the little girl who had nearly collided with them earlier, still chasing about after her brother.

'Gained from...?' Lydia's fingers closed tightly around the rose, tension suffocating its flawed beauty. 'It's just the truth. He's going to have to know it some time! You want to deny it, but you can't, Blaine. I know. I've had a long time to get used to it.'

His mouth twitched into a parody of a smile that died long before it reached his eyes. 'Then grant me the same courtesy,' he said tersely, and swung away from her, over to Liam to tell him that it was time they left.

Things only seemed to deteriorate after that. Despite the efforts he made with Liam, over the next couple of days Blaine's manner became churlish with everyone. Tina scuttled away whenever she saw him coming. Even the middle-aged chauffeur kept his head down and only spoke if he was spoken to, and Judith walked around with that uneasy look about her, and a more than usual lifting of her greying brows when she found herself on the wrong side of his moods.

'Well, you know what's causing all this, don't you, and you know what you must do about it?' Lydia heard Blaine's mother advising strongly one morning as she was passing his study. 'The strain of your foul temper is getting to us all!'

She didn't catch Blaine's swift rejoinder, only knew that it was hot and blistering as she moved rapidly away from the door.

She knew, of course, that Judith was referring to her, and that the woman's continuing opinion—seldom voiced now but ever present—was that Blaine should send her away. And she would have gladly gone, except that Liam's touching entreaties that she stay, that she made being blind easier for him—a fact borne out by his willingness over the past week to learn new skills—kept her there, where Blaine's hard insistence might have failed.

Judith flew home at the end of that week and the following day, Blaine left on business and an overnight stay in New York.

'I don't intend being away from Liam for any longer than I can help,' he told Lydia resolutely as he was leaving. 'I'll be back tomorrow evening, if all goes well.'

And all must have gone well, she thought with a surge of adrenalin the following evening, when she heard the whisper of heavy wheels over the drive and, from the window-seat in the library, where she had been curled up reading, saw Simon bringing the Mercedes back from the airport.

Try though she did, she couldn't stop herself from watching covertly as Blaine stepped out of the car.

In the gathering dusk she could see that he was as immaculately dressed as always, looking fresh and vital, despite having come from some probably very gruelling business meeting.

A man in perfect shape, hair—every bit as dark as hers—perfectly groomed. Blaine Caldwell. Her half-brother, she thought with a bitter, self-derisive little smile. If she'd wanted to, she couldn't have picked a more perfect specimen to be her only blood relative!

And then, as he turned to open the rear passenger door, she realised that he wasn't alone.

Simon had already opened the door on his side for a tall, wiry man about Blaine's age. But it was Shelley who stepped out on the other side, almost into Blaine's arms. Shelley who was laughing and looking up at him as though the very world revolved around him!

Seized by a powerful emotion, Lydia turned angrily away.

'He's your *brother!*' she ground through her clenched

teeth, her anger directed at herself. She had no right to feel so hurt. No right at all!

She was in the living room, tidying one or two things Liam had discarded before he'd gone upstairs, when the others came in.

Shelley sounded in particularly high spirits, Lydia thought, something clutching painfully at her stomach when she turned round and saw the woman—power-dressed, in a figure-hugging black suit and cream blouse—clinging to Blaine's arm like a limpet.

'Hello, Lydia! Still here?' Her effusive greeting held an element, nonetheless, of disappointment. 'I thought you weren't going to be staying long?'

Looking petite between Blaine and the tall man Lydia had seen from the library window, Shelley, she decided, couldn't have made her displeasure plainer if she'd tried.

Feeling like a tall willow beside the curvy blonde, especially as she had chosen to wear a floaty green strappy top with a soft matching skirt, Lydia merely smiled with cool politeness.

'Well, you know how things go, Shelley. More often or not it's the children who dictate the rules.'

Shelley raised one eyebrow as she looked up at the object of her desire. 'And you allow that, Blaine?'

'I told you—Liam had a fall,' he said succinctly, extricating himself from her clinging grasp.

His mood hadn't improved since he had been gone. The impatience in his voice threaded through to infiltrate his movements and his very manner, leaving Lydia craving more than just his curt acknowledgement as he moved across to summon Tina.

'Oh, Dale...' He was halfway over to the fireplace

before remembering to wave an introductory hand towards Lydia.

'I thought you were keeping her to yourself, Blaine,' the other man commented, pulling a wry face at Lydia. 'Although I can't say I would have blamed you if you were.'

Lydia sensed the other woman silently bristling.

'Hardly,' Blaine drawled, without sparing her a glance as he rang the house-bell. 'If you wanted an introduction all you had to do was ask.'

Looking up at the wiry Dale, Lydia shrugged, concealing the sting of Blaine's treatment of her behind an affected smile.

It was out of character, though, for him to forget to observe the basic courtesies, she thought, just as this ongoing dark mood of his was something she had not witnessed before. But then, he had never been confronted with a truth such as she had sprung on him before, she realised bleakly, and tried not to let her own tensions show as the other man shook her hand.

'Lydia Lawrence? Shouldn't I know that name?' It was there, as usual. The puzzling speculation. Even in this quiet, unassuming man who turned out to be Dale Thornton—Blaine's closest associate—and who was shaking his head as though he had made a mistake.

'You mean you haven't heard of Lydia Lawrence? The famous model!' Again Shelley's words were underlaid with something less than friendly. 'At one time you couldn't pick up a paper without reading her name.'

'I'm afraid I've never been much of a newspaper reader,' he said, smiling somewhat apologetically, and Lydia wondered if in fact he didn't remember her at all, or did, and was just being kind.

Refreshments were brought—coffee and light sandwiches, since it seemed the other three had eaten a substantial meal before leaving New York.

Shelley had positioned herself on the sofa next to Blaine, lounging back against its arm so that she could look at him with no pretensions to subtlety, her long legs turned towards him, her body language obvious.

Therefore Dale sat beside Lydia on the opposite sofa, a kindly man, though a little dull, she couldn't help thinking as the evening progressed. Or perhaps it was her fault, she decided, giving him the benefit of the doubt, shamefully aware as she was of her interest lying only in what the other two were saying.

'You know it's no trouble. When has anything you've ever asked me to do, Blaine, been any trouble?'

Shelley thought no one was listening, Lydia surmised. Or if the woman did, then she didn't care.

Her intentions on Blaine were patently obvious tonight, and Lydia could only suppose that Shelley sensed this lurking tension between the man she wanted and his son's nanny and couldn't guess why, since it had to be plain to her that whatever had been between them before was over.

Unable to bear listening to her any longer, and finding Dale's tedious conversation becoming a strain, Lydia went over to put a new disc into the CD player.

She could hear Blaine speaking to Dale now, and Shelley chipping in. When she wasn't fawning over Blaine, she was really a very intelligent woman, Lydia thought, listening to Shelley's knowledgeable input about off-shore tax benefits.

She looked up from the slim silver disc she was trying

to remove from its case, casting a casual glance sideways at the other three.

Shelley and Dale were very animated now, while Blaine was simply listening.

Or was he? Lydia wondered, realising that, just as at other odd times during the evening, until she looked up, his attention had been solely on her.

This time, as she caught him watching her, just for the briefest moment their eyes met in a silent communication—his darkly inscrutable, hers rife with longing—before he glanced swiftly away.

Now he slid his arm along the back of the sofa behind the other woman, his dark head inclining towards her. It was a deliberate exercise, Lydia felt, and probably the most prudent in the circumstances. Nevertheless, it still hurt.

Fumbling with the disc, she gasped as the little silver plate suddenly sprang from her agitated fingers and landed on the richly patterned rug. She picked it up, bent down to put it into the machine, then couldn't get the drawer to close and couldn't understand why.

She was aware of Dale and Shelley arguing amicably about independence for Bermuda, their voices growing louder, then, in sudden contrast, a deeper, softer voice just behind her saying, 'You're getting into a real mess with this, aren't you?'

Blaine's tone was indulgent, but she found she couldn't even look at him now.

'Can you do it?' she uttered with an edge of desperation in her voice.

He did, his fingers long and steady, mocking the furore of emotion she seemed to be embroiled in as he repositioned the disc she had failed properly to align.

'Come and sit down,' he ordered quietly.

She chanced a quick look up at him, and shook her head.

'If you don't mind, I think I'll just go to bed,' she said as Elgar's haunting music started to spill from the system.

For a moment, as he studied her willowy grace beneath the gauzy two-piece, she thought that he was going to argue. But then, surprisingly, he nodded and let her go.

Well, what was she expecting from him? she asked herself torturedly. She wasn't really his employee, as employees went. Nor his guest. Nor even his lover. The complications of their past meant that it was impossible now even to acknowledge a proper sibling status between them.

She was nothing to him, she thought with a dark and aching desolation, and she caught Shelley's look of relief as she offered her apologies to her and Dale and went to bed.

In the darkness of her room she was unable to sleep, tossing and turning like a ship on a merciless sea.

But how could she be awake, she thought, when the water was lapping around her like a deep, dark demon, waiting to swallow her up?

She could feel it seeping through her shoes, creeping up the hem of her dress. Her wedding dress, she realised, looking down.

The water shone like a mirror now, and it was not her reflection gazing back at her, but Shelley's. Shelley on her wedding day, standing beside Blaine.

'No, you can't!'

Her shriek of despair lifted her up into a fevered semi-consciousness.

She'd read something like this once, hadn't she? she thought. In one of the classics? About possessiveness? About a brother and sister? Was she doomed, therefore, to be demented with jealousy over her own brother? As inseparable from him as George Eliot's two star-crossed siblings had been from each other?

Hadn't they drowned at the end? Was that why she kept dreaming about water? But it wasn't reflecting any more. It was dark and murky again and the happy couple had gone. Where had they gone?

'Blaine!'

Desperately, she plunged into the depths, the dress clinging to her now, hampering her progress, seeming to pull her down with invisible hands. 'Blaine! Where are you?' She lashed out, fighting the suffocating black body of water. 'Blaine!'

'I'm here.'

She couldn't see him. 'Don't leave me!'

'I won't leave you.' His voice seemed to tremble with suppressed emotion.

Where was he? She peered through the frightening darkness, but still couldn't see him.

'Hold me. Make everything right.'

'Everything is all right.' From somewhere his words came softly and soothingly. 'Hush! You were just dreaming.'

And then there was peace. Such perfect peace and warmth, and she was breaking through the surface to-wards a beckoning sun.

'Come on, Lydia, wake up.' She felt someone shaking

her now, very gently, by the shoulder. 'Come on, it's only a dream.'

A dream?

Her eyelashes flickered open, her consciousness returning to the sight of Blaine sitting there on the edge of her bed.

A dream, he had said. Only it wasn't.

She was sensitive to the hand that still lay on her shoulder, sensitive to its warmth, its consoling strength.

'Are you...all right now?' His voice was tight with restraint.

Still gripped by the imagery of her dream, she couldn't answer, only aware of how swiftly he withdrew his hand as she pulled herself up onto her pillows.

He was still wearing the clothes he had been wearing earlier. The top button of his shirt was unfastened, though, and his hair was dishevelled, as though he had been raking his fingers through it while he read or worked or whatever it was that had kept him from going to bed.

In the soft light from the lamp, she saw the damp streak above his unshaven jaw. Her own face was wet, she realised now, with the tears she had shed so bitterly in her sleep.

Had he held her? Dear God! Just once! Despite all that she could never be to him, had he held her?

Her eyes lifted in aching turmoil to his. His features were shadowed, pinched from some deep and private emotion, and his own eyes were dark with concern. Brotherly concern...

'No!'

She screamed it at him—at the universe—a rejection of everything fraternal and hopelessly final.

There was a commotion across the landing, the jangle of the bead curtain from someone hurrying across the top of the stairs.

'What's wrong?'

'I heard somebody yelling. Is everything all right?'

It was Shelley, sounding puzzled, jealously suspicious, and Dale, too, just behind her. They were both in their nightclothes.

'It's all right.' The bed depressed as Blaine stood up and looked down at Lydia. It was a lean, desolate look before his chest lifted and fell again with hard, exercised discipline. 'It's OK,' he reassured the others, with more than a hint of impatience, as though he somehow found their intrusion tiresome, adding with casual yet startling sincerity, 'Just my little sister having one of her bad dreams.'

'Your sister?' It was Shelley, leaving Lydia to whatever horrors the night chose to inflict upon her, following him now as he pushed out of the room. 'Your *sister*? Blaine, you're joking?' Her voice was fading along the landing. 'Blaine! Wait a minute…'

Dale shrugged, looking decidedly uncomfortable in hideously striped pyjamas.

'Oh, well…I'll say goodnight, then,' he murmured puzzled and embarrassed, but too polite to enquire what Blaine had meant.

Alone, Lydia closed her eyes, letting her head drop back against the padded satin of the headboard.

So he had said it. Admitted it. Accepted it. But why now? she wondered, still stunned from the shock of his finally making it public. Was it to stamp the unwelcome fact on his brain once and for all? Or was it a decision made merely for the other woman's benefit? To try and safeguard whatever future he thought he might have with Shelley?

Lydia knew she was being just a little bit unreasonable, thinking of him in such calculating terms. After all, there could be no future for them together, in any capacity.

Perhaps he'd realised it at last, she thought, catching her breath as the only thing she was drowning in now was her suffocating emotion. At least now perhaps he'd realise that they couldn't go on living under the same roof.

Therefore, the very next day, though she hated leaving Liam, she packed up her belongings, checked that there was an available seat on a UK flight out of Bermuda, and that very same evening flew home.

CHAPTER NINE

LYDIA considered the familiar face of the model gazing up at her from the glossy cover.

Too much blusher, perhaps? Cheekbones far too over-emphasised? But not one tiny line in sight!

At thirty-two, she could still hold her own against girls half her age, she thought with a self-mocking little smile, although she had only agreed to let the magazine use her as a favour to Gary.

He had been having a tough time when Diane, his resident model girlfriend, pulled out of their long-standing relationship and he'd had to find exorbitant funds to buy her share of their home.

'This new mag's running an article on child-minding and British nannies,' he had informed her. Then, almost beseechingly, had added, 'They'll pay me a fortune if I can come up with a photograph of you. It's the one break I could do with, and with you on the cover of the launch edition—'

'I know. Sales will rocket.' She wasn't being immodest. Just totally factual. Over the years, magazines, fashion houses and newspapers still approached her, keen for a glimpse of the face and figure which, she was beginning to dread, would always attract attention. 'No, Gary.' She had been adamant.

She had enough money to live on, an average-sized comfortable house in the city suburbs. And, having invested what money she hadn't put into the agency

wisely, from her old modelling days, she had a very
secure future.

'Please,' Gary had persisted. 'It could mean the difference for *me* between a bed to sleep on and bank-
ruptcy.'

She hadn't realised that. She owed him, after all, she
thought, for taking care of her when she had had her
nervous breakdown and providing her with that job in
South Africa.

Consequently, when she'd found out the sort of
money the magazine was offering, she'd agreed to do it,
as well as a short interview, insisting that it was only to
promote child-minding agencies and that there be no ref-
erence to her old modelling career. But it was only to
help Gary, and she'd told him so, then sunk the entire
profit from her own fee into a well-known charity for
the blind.

The truth was that during her short time in Bermuda
Blaine's son had stolen her heart. She had written to him
once or twice at the Bermuda address, inwardly denying
that she was in any way trying to prompt some sort of
response from Blaine. But although she'd received a reply on cassette tape from Liam, in which he informed
her he was now back home in Surrey, there had been no
news from his father. She knew, though, that Liam must
have enlisted Blaine's help in getting that tape to her,
and somehow that made his own lack of communication
even harder to bear.

He was being sensible, she told herself. Following the
only course he could. And on top of that, of course, there
was Shelley, casually mentioned in Liam's letter, but
very much in evidence nonetheless.

'How can anyone be so miserable and look so utterly

beautiful on it?' Heather marvelled from behind her desk one morning, wriggling her loose silk blouse down over rather generous hips as she eyed Lydia's pencil-straight skirt and clinging top that enhanced the enviable slenderness of her figure.

'I'm not miserable, Heather,' Lydia told her resolutely. She had to keep telling herself that, otherwise she would crack up as she had done before, and she couldn't. She just wouldn't allow herself to be destroyed by her feelings for a man whom it was entirely wrong to love as she'd done the last time. 'And just for once don't try telling me what I want or how I'm feeling.'

Beneath her swept-up red hair, Heather's expression was wry as Lydia came around her own desk and sat down.

'Ooh-ooh! Just because my attempts to play cupid didn't work out. Perhaps the arrows were a little rusty—'

'Rusty?' The eyes Lydia turned on the amply endowed Heather were heavy with repressed emotion, a heaviness that only enhanced the beauty to which the woman had been referring. 'They were poison-tipped!'

'Oh, come on, Lyddie! You know I only ever mean well.'

'Well, don't,' Lydia advised without looking at her, picking up her pen to show her colleague that she was serious. Sometimes with Heather, she thought, it was the only way.

The fact was that she hadn't told her partner, or anyone else, the real reason why she had made such an unexpected departure from Bermuda two months ago. That Blaine Caldwell was really her half-brother. She didn't want to acknowledge it. Or these feelings that still seemed to crucify her with their intensity. She wanted

to be free of them. To know a day when she could think
of him with only a warm, and sisterly affection. The way
she should be thinking of him. And knew, deep in her
heart, that she was crying for the moon.

'So how's Gary?' She was brought back to the present
by Heather asking, obviously getting the message that
any conversation to do with Blaine Caldwell was entirely banned.

'Well, you know Gary.'

Heather did. Lydia had mentioned him often enough.
Surprisingly, though, her colleague had long since ac-
cepted that friendship was all there was between Lydia
and the thirty-five-year-old photographer, for which
Lydia was eternally grateful. She had had enough of
Heather's matchmaking attempts over the years.

'He's throwing a party tonight to show everyone that
he doesn't care about Diane leaving—but he does,'
Lydia enlarged sympathetically, only having accepted
his invitation to give him some moral support. She hated
parties at the best of times, but nowadays she felt more
lonely socialising than spending whole evenings alone.

Gary met her at the door that evening with what she
knew was an air of totally forced gaiety.

'Come in! Come in!' he welcomed her enthusiasti-
cally, sporting new blond streaks in his rather mousy
hair, the customary jeans and T-shirt looking—uncus-
tomarily—as if they had been slept in. 'The party's refused to begin without my favourite girl!'

'Oh, Gary!' Lydia hid her own cares behind a bright
smile and returned his hug.

He'd been drinking—and quite heavily, she guessed,
which he never did unless he had problems with Diane,

something which had been occurring with increasing frequency over the past couple of years. She could smell the whisky on his breath.

'You watch your intake,' she advised, her tone caring and soft as he drew her into the rather trendy, upmarket apartment. 'Otherwise we'll be carrying you off to bed.'

Gary grinned. 'Which I still have—thanks to you,' he reminded her, appraising her simple black dress with its double shoelace shoulder-straps that exposed the pale gold of her skin, the sheer barely black stockings and strappy high-heeled shoes she'd worn to complement it.

'You look stunning tonight—but then I've never known you look anything else,' he said, with his arm around her shoulders. 'Hair shining like a raven's wing. Smoky-grey eyelids. Perfectly kissable pink mouth.' Ignoring her amiable protest that he was going over the top, he drew her into the circle of friends and acquaintances who were standing around chatting, saying ebulliently, 'Meet the most benevolent, beautiful model I've ever worked with. Don't you think she's beautiful?'

'Gary,' Lydia whispered, embarrassed, recognising some of the faces from the fashion world she'd once inhabited.

Some of the women laughed. There was a murmur of agreement from most of the men. And then someone responded with, 'What are you trying to do, Gary, prove a point?'

Because he was, Lydia thought. He'd do anything rather than let anyone know he was pining for Diane.

As he muttered something under his breath and left her side—clearly irked that someone might have guessed the truth—Lydia was left to face a barrage of comments and speculative questions.

'That cover shot of you was something else! You barely look a day over twenty!'

'Did you know sales of that mag are exceeding all expectations?'

'Does this mean we'll be seeing more of you?'

'I do hope so. It was a sad loss to the industry when Lydia Lawrence closed her portfolio on the world.'

Some of them were her friends, and entirely genuine. Others were simply gushing, caught up in a business that could be as cut-throat as it was glamorous.

'Thanks.' She smiled her appreciation for those compliments that were meant. 'But don't think I'm making a comeback. It was a one-off. Nothing more.'

She lost herself then in the superficial business of polite conversation, hating every moment, her smile so forced it made her jaw ache.

It was almost a relief, eventually, to slip away to the bathroom, where she retouched her lipstick before deciding to find Gary to tell him she was going home.

She hadn't seen him for half an hour or more, not since he'd rushed off to take a phone call in the privacy of the bedroom.

Now, as she passed the door to that room, which was open enough for her to realise that he wasn't speaking to anyone, tentatively she knocked.

His sighed 'Yes?' brought her in to find him sitting on the end of the large metal-framed bed, shoulders sagging beneath the crumpled T-shirt, arms hanging limply between his legs.

'That was Diane,' he said without any prompting, when he realised it was Lydia. His speech was slightly slurred. 'She wants to come back.' He dropped his head into his hands in a gesture of total despair. 'After all she's done to me, she wants to come back.'

'Oh, Gary.' Dropping down beside him, Lydia put her arms around him. She knew something of the pain he was going through. Wasn't she trying to come to terms with loving someone she should never have loved until it was driving her insane?

'I'll have her back, of course,' he admitted in a tone of hopeless resignation. 'But not until I've shown her what sort of man she's dealing with. I'll show her!'

'Of course you will,' Lydia smiled, kissing his fashionably unshaven cheek, because she knew Gary was too soft ever to hurt anyone.

And with her temple pressed to his in companionable comfort, she was as unaware as he was of the sudden increase in the volume of laughter and music as someone pushed open the door until the abrasive masculine tones drifted towards them.

'Is this a private party, or can anyone join in?'

'Blaine!' Lydia jumped up, his name inaudible on her lips, her colour draining as though someone had pulled a plug.

He looked powerful and imposing in a dark lounge suit that seemed to grant him a sophistication over every other casually dressed individual at the party, and his face was set in hard, purposeful lines.

In spite of that, though, and his rather disadvantageous position, it didn't stop Gary from demanding, 'Who the hell are you?'

Blaine's gaze was riveted on Lydia, and not just her face, but seeming to touch all of her, sapping her strength—her very life, it seemed—from every cell in her body.

'I could ask you the same thing.'

Gary rose rather unsteadily to his feet. 'Oh, you could, could you?' He swayed a little as he stuck his chin in the air. 'Well, it just so happens I live here.'

'So you're Gary.' Blaine's mouth pulled down grimly one side. 'Well, Gary, would you mind taking yourself off and playing the friendly host to a few of your other neglected guests? I want to talk to Lydia.'

Affronted, Gary took a brave step forward. 'Now just a minute…'

'No, this instant.' Blaine's tone brooked no argument as he strode into the room, that total self-assurance causing Gary to visibly shrink. Even a larger man would have been daunted by it, Lydia decided. And Blaine towered over Gary by a good head.

'Who is this?' The photographer nevertheless found some confidence to demand. An alcohol-induced confidence, Lydia was sure. 'Who the hell does he think he is, coming in here and acting like he's some sort of wronged husband?'

Stunned by Blaine's sheer nerve, but more from the overwhelming shock of seeing him there, Lydia found it almost too much to speak.

'Try my brother,' she uttered in a tremulous yet no less defiant voice at last.

Gary screwed up his eyes. 'Your brother? You haven't got a brother.' He looked unsteadily from Blaine to Lydia and back to Blaine again, standing there in the contemporary luxury of the bedroom that reflected Diane's ultra-modern taste. 'Bit possessive for a brother, isn't he?' he remarked, and took a step back as Blaine advanced, clearly undeterred.

'Yes, as a matter of fact, I am!'

Recovering herself now, Lydia moved towards Blaine, her head held challengingly high above the exposed column of her throat.

'What right have you got—coming in here pushing people around?' she enquired sharply. To be alone with Blaine was the last thing she wanted. She couldn't cope with that. 'Stay if you want to, Gary.'

'Not if you know what's best for you, Gary.'

Gary's face suffused with hot colour at the soft delivery of Blaine's recommendation. 'Are you threatening me?' he queried, his mouth turning aggressive.

Blaine's smile was purely superficial. His tone, though, was steely as he said, 'I'm sure we're both sensible enough adults not to have to stoop to those sort of tactics.'

'Now just—'

'Gary! Blaine! Stop it! *Stop it!*' Lydia's cry was desperate. She just couldn't stand there and see the two people she cared about most at loggerheads with each other. 'You'd better go, Gary,' she advised with gentle reluctance now, deciding that any resistance from either of them would be fruitless against Blaine's determination.

He looked at her, then back at Blaine. 'Are you sure?' he asked, his challenging snarl only half-hearted in view of the older man's dominant stance.

'Yes.' Her hand on his arm was more than willing him to go for his own sake. 'Please…'

'All right, then.' With a grudging look at Blaine he started towards the door. Beyond it the party throbbed, people laughed. Music drifted in. 'If you need me, call me,' he said.

'I'll see she does.' Blaine's tone was impatient. 'But I don't think it will be this side of tomorrow.'

'What did you mean by that?' Lydia demanded, backing away from him as he flung the door closed behind the other man, muting the lively tempo of the party.

'Meaning we've got a lot to talk about,' he said.

Lydia shook her head, her eyes wary. 'I don't think so, Blaine,' she uttered, with her heart pounding through a deep well of hopelessness. 'How did you find me, anyway? How did you know I was here?'

'Heather,' he explained at the same instant that she guessed. 'When you weren't at home I telephoned your office, in case you might have been working late. She was still there and was more than obliging in letting me know that you'd be here.'

Which she would have been, Lydia thought distractedly, especially if he'd given his name.

'You shouldn't have come.' Anguish trembled through her voice. 'You know it's best that we never see each other again.'

His lips thinned and he seemed to grow pale, his gaze tugging over the strained contours of her face. 'Is that what you really want?' he pressed quietly.

'Yes.' She forced herself to say it.

'Like you really wanted Gary What's-his-name?'

'Yes!' She flung it at him, colouring singeing her cheeks. 'And you had no right to drive him away!'

Perhaps he would believe it, and then he'd go, she thought hectically, terrified of the feelings his mere presence evoked.

But he just laughed and said, 'I'm only doing what I didn't do the last time, Lydia. I'm not making the same mistake again.'

Fear clouded her eyes, darkening their turbulent sapphire. 'What do you mean?' she whispered, taking another step back.

'There's only one man you want in your life—that you've ever wanted in your life—and that's me!' he said, jabbing a thumb against the silky whiteness of his shirt.

'You're crazy, Blaine!' It came out on a sob. 'You can't spend your life playing the possessive brother. You've got to let me go.'

'No!' It was a hard negation, one which brought the torturous anguish welling up inside of her.

'You can't accept it, can you?' she sobbed. 'Like you refused to accept Liam's blindness. Staying away from him because you couldn't face up—'

Suddenly he had closed the gap between them and his hands were on her shoulders. She could feel the vibes of his anger running down his fingers, unintentionally hurting her where they dug into her bare flesh.

'I stayed away from him because I couldn't bear to face what I'd done to him. What my stupid and selfish motives for marrying Sharon had done to him—and to her. Because I married her when I was still so crazily demented with my feelings for you. Because I wanted to show you. Because I wanted to hurt you. Because I couldn't forget you—even up until the afternoon she died!'

'Stop it!' She clamped her hands over her ears.

'No!' Roughly his fingers bit into her wrists, dragging her hands mercilessly down.

'Oh, Blaine, please… This can't happen between us!' Dear God! What was wrong with her that these feelings were so strong?

Her head started to swim—not with alcohol, because

she had scarcely touched a drop, but with the ravages of emotion that were suddenly proving all too much for her to bear. The thrill and torture of seeing him. The sick, sick longing. The fearful conviction now that there really *was* something wrong with her…

For a moment her knees seemed to buckle, only that strong clasp on her lower arms preventing her from sinking in to the weakening, bone-melting haze.

'For heaven's sake, Lydia!' Blaine's voice came distantly, as though through a thick fog. 'What do I have to say to even start to convince you? I'm not your brother! Have you got that?' And imperatively, yet slowly, as though he were speaking to an idiot, or someone not wholly in command of the language, he reiterated, *'I'm not your brother!'*

CHAPTER TEN

HER senses returning, Lydia looked, disbelieving, up into the hard contours of his face. And again he said, 'I'm not your brother. Do you really think the attraction between us would be this powerful if I were?'

Feeling the dizziness receding, she pulled out of his grasp, backing into the crimson of Diane's flamboyantly painted dressing table.

'That's only because of the past! What we thought we could be! You can't pretend your father lied and reject our relationship like that!'

'Can't I?' Some harsh emotion caused deep grooves around his eyes and mouth, suddenly making him look his full forty years. 'Because he did.'

Lydia frowned. 'Did what?'

'Lied.'

Mirthlessly, she laughed. 'And you can prove that?'

'I know, it is bloody laughable, isn't it?' He was angry now. Really angry. 'That one person can manipulate so many lives for his own selfish motives. But that's what he did, Lydia. Regardless of what he thought about you, he wanted that merger with Hilliers above anything else, and my marriage to Sharon was all part of the package he'd been hoping for for a long time. As far as he was concerned, no one but Hiller's daughter was right for his only son. Then you came on the scene and put a spanner in the works, and when he checked you out and found you'd never known who your father was, it was like a

169

ripe apple falling into his lap. He went out of his way
to try and break us up and to make sure you never came
near me again—and succeeded!'

'What do you mean?' The furrow between her eyes
deepened. Why was he talking like this? What was it he
was trying to say?

'I'm not your brother,' he stressed for the fourth time.
'Oh, Father might have had an affair with your mother.
He might not have lied about that. But even if he didn't,
there's still no way you could ever have been my sister.'

Lydia's face looked gaunt and pale beneath the dark
shiny crown of her hair. 'What are you talking about?'
she breathed.

'My father was infertile,' he stated crisply.

Lydia stared at him, saying nothing until his words
finally sank in.

'But—but he had you,' she reminded him with dismissive emphasis.

'Mother had me,' he corrected.

Lydia's eyes widened. 'You mean...' She hesitated.
Surely the aloof and very proper Judith Caldwell hadn't
had a clandestine affair?

'No, it's not what you're thinking,' Blaine assured
her, seeming to read her thoughts. 'When they found out
my father couldn't produce children, my mother took
medical steps to enable her to conceive me. They agreed
that any child of their marriage should be part of at least
one of them, rather than a stranger's child—through
adoption. I don't know who my father was. A medical
student. Probably someone of the right physical and
mental calibre. Isn't that what they look for in these
cases?'

Numbed by the sheer impact of all he was telling her,

she was only half aware of the music and conversation going on in the rest of the apartment, of a car wending its way along the road outside.

She lifted her face to his. Was it true? All of it? Because if it was…

'Did—did Judith tell you all this?' she enquired falteringly, hardly daring to believe it, what it could all mean.

'Who else?'

'But why?' Disbelief was giving way to other emotions, hard and questioning. 'And why didn't she tell us that night in the library? She backed up your father's story.' Anger was rising through the shock which, up until now, had prevented her from feeling anything else. 'Why, Blaine? She knew what we felt about each other. Didn't she? Wasn't that why she was so keen that I come home?'

Although if the woman had known all along that they weren't related, why should it have mattered to her one way or the other? Lydia wondered injuredly, bewildered.

Blaine's gaze lifted past her shoulder to the window, as though he were looking for some justifiable answer in the darkness beyond it, his attention returning to her on what sounded like a deeply regretful sigh.

'She was unhappy about you being there. Not because she thought you were my sister—quite the opposite,' he said. 'But don't think too badly of her, Lydia. She had a burden to bear, too. She was torn between being open with us and complying with my father's wishes.'

'What wishes?' Lydia queried poignantly. The man had as good as ruined her life, and his wife had done nothing but support him in it!

'Apparently a promise she felt she had to keep and

which she made to him shortly before he died. According to my mother, he wanted to believe I was his child until he'd convinced himself of it. He wanted everything for me—so I suppose I should be tolerant—but he went too far, and I suppose eventually he blamed himself for the way my life turned out. He confessed everything to my mother during that last conversation he was able to have with her. The one thing, though, that he made her promise was that she would never tell me I wasn't his son.'

And she had promised. She must have, Lydia realised. And, of course, to tell them the truth—that they weren't related in any way—would have meant breaking it...

She could see also now why Judith had been so keen to avoid telling Liam anything about her, even though she didn't yet feel ready to forgive her. Because if she had, it would have meant simply compounding her husband's lies.

Eventually she asked, 'What made her break her promise?'

Beneath the immaculate dark suit, one broad shoulder lifted slightly.

'Probably the fact that I've been so impossible since you came back into my life, but particularly after you'd walked out of it again. I destroyed every photograph I'd ever had of you—both here and in Bermuda—and, as if to taunt me, there you were again, the cover girl on every news-stand, at every station, in every airport. Did you do it to taunt me, Lydia?'

His eyes were dark, so tortured that she wanted to run to him. But all she said quietly was, 'No, I did it to help...a friend.' She didn't want to mention Gary's name. Not here. Not now.

He frowned, but gave a half-nod, content for the time being with that.

'Anyway,' he went on, 'she decided that my happiness—and yours—had to come before any promise she'd made to my father. It hurt her to do it. I don't really know how much. But she adored my father—in spite of the way he treated her—the way she *knew* he treated her—with his extra-marital affairs. So there you have it, Lydia. If you want me for a big brother, then I'll get the hell out of your life. But if you want *me*—'

A sob escaped her. 'Want you?' She could scarcely speak. All that she could think about was that he wasn't her brother! That he had never been her brother! All the wasted time and anguish. The years when she'd believed that they could never be together...

'Oh, Blaine...!'

Tears filled her eyes as those grey ones of Blaine's willed her to come to him. With a stifled sound she ran towards him, but the embrace she craved was cruelly curtailed by the door suddenly flying open.

Gary burst in, looking suspiciously at the two of them, his attention going from Blaine's hand clutching Lydia's elbow to her seemingly distressed face.

Anger twisted his mouth above the heavily stubbled jaw, and he looked ready to take on Blaine and all the world if need be.

'You're not her brother. You're Blaine...Caldwell, aren't you?' he slurred censoriously.

'That's right.' In spite of everything, Blaine looked remarkably composed.

'Yeah. The sw-swine who ditched her before to marry someone else.' He looked at Lydia, at those beautiful high cheekbones, still moist with emotion, and de-manded, 'Have you been up...setting her again?'

'Gary, please...' Lydia beseeched him, attempting to pull away from Blaine, who had other ideas and kept a firm grip on her elbow. 'It isn't what it looks like.'

Gary grunted. 'No?'

Surprisingly, all Blaine said drily in response was, 'Sleep it off, old chap,' as he urged Lydia past him to-wards the door.

Poor Gary, she thought. He really was the worse for drink. In the morning he'd have a head and a half and wouldn't remember a thing.

At that moment, however, unwisely, the photographer seemed determined to provoke Blaine, and behind them she heard him racing on, 'OK. You think I'm drunk, do you? Well, p'rhaps I am. But I've got scruples—which is more than you've ever had, Blaine Caldwell! There's a name for...rats like you, who land a girl in the soup and then leave so-some other man to pick up the pieces.' He wagged a finger at Lydia, who had stopped, like Blaine, and was staring incredulously at Gary as though she couldn't believe what he was actually saying. 'You didn't realise I knew, did you? But I recognised the signs and sus...pected that that was what had nearly driven you off your head. And *you*...' He lunged towards Blaine, lost his balance and only saved himself by bump-ing into the soft back of a pink velour easy chair. 'You should learn how to treat women, you should.'

'Well, thanks for the advice, Gary,' Blaine responded. sounding unperturbed, but Lydia could feel the bunching of muscle in his arm as he thrust her out of the door.

She felt exposed and vulnerable suddenly, feeling Blaine's tense silence like that between lightning and the inevitable roll of thunder as he ushered her through the trendy ambience of the apartment.

People parted, making way for them before the determination on Blaine's face, as though recognising a force that could control tides.

Like an automaton she smiled at the guests who said goodnight to them, absently aware of how much female interest Blaine was attracting as she was led, almost blindly by him, to the front door.

'What exactly did he mean by that?'

There it was. The inescapable question. His voice strung with a tense urgency as, with an arm around her waist, he guided her swiftly over the steps to his waiting car.

It was low-slung and sleek, in dark green, parked just along the road from the modern apartment block.

When she didn't answer, he merely opened the passenger door for her, before coming around the bonnet and sliding in on the other side.

'Well?' he prompted, looking at her across the shadowy interior.

Lydia took a deep breath, steeling herself now to tell him the truth.

'I was pregnant,' was all she said in a whisper, staring out through the windscreen. Pregnant with the child of a man it had been totally legitimate to love all along— a child conceived seemingly out of a dream. Because when she had slept with him that night—unintentionally, and for the first time—she'd been a virgin still—afraid, as he had reminded her that day in Bermuda, of following the same path her mother had taken. Because he had been right when he'd said that she would never *consciously* commit herself to letting it happen, when he'd gone along with her vehement denial, that day on the beach, that anything more than chaste kisses had passed between them all those years ago.

Newly engaged, staying with his parents for the first time, she'd sensed the disapproval in Blaine's father and had tried telling herself it was entirely in her own mind. But that night her doubts and fears had given rise to the vivid and grotesque dreams that she had been prone to all her life, and her cries had brought Blaine into her room.

She had fallen asleep in his arms where, deep in the depths of some erotic dream, he had been making love to her. Only somewhere during that endless night the dream had blended with reality, and he had taken her through the gates of a paradisiacal experience which, in the morning, when she woke to find him gone, had seemed only imagined and surreal.

She hadn't realised that it was his father's doing that he had gone away that day—called away on supposedly urgent business. She'd been too preoccupied with her own starry-eyed dreams.

Only the dreams had turned into a nightmare of the ugliest proportions when the man had summoned her to his office the following afternoon.

Oh, Blaine's father had never realised the degree of devastation he had caused her, she thought, shivering from the brutality of his deception. She wondered if he would even have cared if he had.

'I lost it,' she said quietly, and a silent tear slid down the side of her nose. 'The day after I'd read that you and Sharon were going to have a baby.'

Now she could openly mourn the child she had lost with such heart-rending feelings of relief and guilt and hopeless desolation at the time. Such feelings that had tortured her until she had cracked. And then, after Gary had nursed her through that breakdown, she had at least been able to pretend that it had never happened, that she had never met Blaine Caldwell, let alone fallen deeply in love with him.

'It was all I had left of you,' she uttered, with all the depth of her feelings for him. 'And I couldn't let it go.'

'Oh, my love…'

He was reaching for her, pulling her into his arms, his lips kissing away the tears that ran down her cheeks, that were being swept away on a tide of sensation.

The warmth of his body was spreading an answering warmth in herself. She turned her face to his, desperate for the feel of his lips on hers, and heard him curse as a car swung in to the space in front of them, its headlights glaring, its horn tooting loudly as the illuminating lights invaded their privacy.

'Let's get the hell out of here,' Blaine rasped, releasing her.

He started the engine then, and drove like a demon through the busy suburbs, out into the merciful darkness of the countryside.

Neither said a word, as though even verbal communication was too intrusive on their pressing need to be alone together.

When Blaine pulled off the road at last, it was to swing onto the drive of his home.

Someone had told her he'd moved after Sharon's accident, and she was glad. There would be no ghosts of his marriage here.

It was a large house, she noticed, surrounded by rambling grounds as far as she could make out through the shadows, but she scarcely took any of it in. She was held in a state of indescribable euphoria.

Blaine was not her brother. Blaine was her lover. The man she adored. Whom it was perfectly right and natural and permissible to adore.

'Come on,' was all he said as he took the keys out of the ignition.

He didn't reach for her, though, after he had come round and opened her door, as she'd imagined he might, only to guide her towards the house.

Perhaps he was determined there would be no more interruptions. At any rate, it was an aphrodisiac of sorts, this denial, she decided. They had waited this long. There was no need to rush things.

So little need, she thought with an anticipation that would make her laugh at herself afterwards, that she went through the door he opened as though in a hypnotic trance.

There was no light burning in the hall, and he didn't switch one on.

'Where's Liam?' she whispered.

And he answered. 'With his grandmother.'

Behind her, she heard him close the door, shutting out the night and the world.

Her eyes adjusted to the darkness and she turned round, her breath catching from this long-awaited and utterly tender intimacy with him.

'Lydia…'

It was a rough whisper from him and that was all. No more words. No more wanting. No more waiting.

They moved towards each other in the same instant, reaching for one another, their mouths meeting in a desperate need that could no longer be denied.

Greedily her hands explored the warm, exciting power of him, her trembling fingers losing themselves in the sensuality of his dark hair.

He shaped her to his body, moulding every curve and angle and plane to the dominating strength of his, while his lips moved from hers with a hunger that couldn't be contained, tasting her cheek, her jaw, her throat.

'Oh, God,' he groaned. 'I've wanted this for so long.'

She strained against him, gasping her pleasure as she revelled in hearing him say it.

'Tell me again,' she pleaded, drunk with the feel and the sound and the scent of him.

'I want you!' It was a growled statement before his mouth clamped urgently over hers again.

His possessiveness excited her, her need of this man whom she had loved for so long an unbearable ecstasy that fed itself, driving her mindless with desire as he slid the back zipper of her dress down and pushed the thin straps aside for his lips to trace the creamy slope of her shoulder, his teeth sensuously nipping her soft flesh.

'Will you come to bed with me?' Passion choked the words he uttered against her throat, words that caught at her heart even as they excited her.

He had to be in no doubt about it, and yet he still asked!

'Just try and stop me,' she whispered, shuddering from the ecstasy of his touch.

He picked her up then, although their lips and hands still clung as he carried her upstairs, so that there was no interlude between those first frenzied kisses in the hall and the beautiful experience that enveloped them both in his bed.

His hands were familiar and yet new to her, but unlike

that surreal episode of before this was real and absolute, sharpening all her senses to every sensation.

'You're mine. All mine,' she heard him whisper as his lips and hands adored her body, more possessive than at any time before. 'Not Gary's, or any other man's. Mine. Do you understand?'

She smiled behind the sensual weight of her closed lids. 'I've never been anyone else's,' she whispered, and heard his sharp intake of breath.

Had he imagined she had been? How could she have been, when she was bound to him? When she had always been bound to him, she realised—from the beginning of time—and with bonds far greater than those of any brother or sister.

'Blaine…' In her dreams she had remembered him as tender. Now, even in his passion, time had made him a lover of mind-blowing consideration, but their mutual hunger was too demanding to remain unsated for long.

'Blaine.' She sighed his name again and arched towards him, her world, her universe, her lover.

It was the ultimate capitulation, aching as she was to be part of him, and now with a groan he accepted it, stretched to the boundaries of his control.

And then the world ceased to exist, and all the years that she had been without him. They were lovers in mind and body, as they had been born to be, and the result was an outpouring of emotion that sent shudders through her slender body as the last waves of their desire ebbed away.

'Don't,' he murmured, kissing the tears that strayed down the curve of her so photogenic face, touched by the soft light of a landing lamp she hadn't even been aware of him switching on.

'I can't help it,' she sniffed with a tremulous smile.

There was a smear on his cheek, a damp streak that brought a memory surging to the forefront of her mind.

He had held her before, hadn't he? When she had had that nightmare in Bermuda? Then she had had to clench her fist to stop herself...

Freely now, she reached up and lightly traced the warm, slightly rough damp skin with the back of her hand.

'I love you,' she whispered.

He caught her slim fingers within the hard bronze of his, uncurling their delicate structure to press his lips to her soft warm palm.

'And if I said I love you, it wouldn't be enough,' he murmured hoarsely. 'But...'

He sat up then with a deep sigh which, with that one lingering word, sent an ominous little shudder through her.

'But what?' she whispered, raising herself up on an elbow. She couldn't see his face clearly, only the dark, tense lines of his profile.

'I can't ask you to marry me now,' he said brutally.

Lydia's heart seemed to stand still. Of course. There had been no promises. Those he had made to her all those years ago were null and void now.

'I can't even ask you to live with me,' he supplemented with a profound regret in his voice, those broad shoulders slightly hunched away from her.

'Why not?' she murmured, running a finger over the smooth velvet of his back, and dreaded the answer, because she couldn't even begin to imagine what he was going to say. That he had been driven by passion? That physically he had ached for her for so long that anything he had said or done, out of that need for her, he couldn't hold himself wholly responsible for? That he had made other promises? Other commitments? 'Is it because of Shelley?'

She felt his back straighten, felt the sudden tightening of the muscles beneath those firm shoulder-blades.

'Shelley?'

Lydia swallowed. Was he trying to break it to her gently? Was that why he was pretending to sound just a little bit surprised?

'I know how you feel about her,' she said quietly, trying to keep her tone even, trying not to sound as though she wanted to scream out that how could he possibly have made love to her with such infinite tenderness if another woman had the ruling power in his heart. 'I know why you had to let her think I was your sister when we were in Bermuda. I can understand why you let yourself get involved. But you were involved with her anyway, weren't you? When you found out about me—that I was—that you thought I was—your sister— you went to her, didn't you? It was her you spent the night with, wasn't it, when you didn't come home?'

Quickly he turned onto his side to face her. 'No, it wasn't.' His denial was too swift and hard to be doubted. 'I simply drove around the island for a couple of hours and then spent the night in the car, parked on the approach to one of the South Shore beaches! And you don't know how I feel about her, because all we've ever had is the promise of a good physical relationship which never actually got off the ground—partly because I've always been rather dubious about mixing business with pleasure, but mainly because, although she is a very attractive woman, she isn't one I would want to make a lasting commitment with, and I didn't want to be that unfair to her—or myself. And the reason I said what I did that night—to her and Thornton—about us being brother and sister—was because I thought that if I finally let it out into the open I could begin to believe it myself, although I don't think it ever really allowed itself to sink in. Maybe my subconscious knew all the time that there was no way you could ever be anything to me but my friend and my lover...'

Lydia sucked in her breath as he allowed one hand to shape the smooth contour of her waist, her hip, the sensitive firmness of her thigh.

'I know I'm going to have to do some explaining to them,' he said, 'and heaven only knows what I'm going to say!' He gave a little chuckle.

Seeing him more relaxed, less serious than he had been a moment ago, softly, her tone tentatively teasing, she asked, 'So why won't you marry me?'

And knew the answer, even before he said, 'Because of Liam. It wouldn't be fair to expect you to take him on with all his problems.'

Now it was her turn to draw herself up swiftly, and, unashamed, she gazed down at him in her glorious nakedness.

'Don't you think I should have a chance to decide whether it would be unfair or not? I love Liam, and I think he likes me too, whether you do or not. In fact he asked me to marry you that day I took him to the Botanical Gardens.'

Blaine laughed softly. 'That's right, he did, didn't he?' But then, in a more pressing tone, he went on, 'Do you mean you'd be prepared to accept him as your own—

with all the difficulties it could mean…?' Disbelief seemed to choke his words.

'Only if you promise that we could have a baby as soon as we were married—or at least start making one,' she said rather quaintly, with a sad note creeping into her voice as she thought of the child that should have been theirs—the dream-child—who had been destined never to be. 'And any difficulties we meet we can overcome—just as long as we're together. I just want Liam to have his wish—for a little sister or brother.'

A hand at the nape of her neck drew her head gently down to his.

'Half-brother,' he whispered against her mouth.

'Don't,' she pleaded as that accurate but oh, so detested noun sent a swift sharp twinge of emotion through her. 'Never say that—even if it's right. I can't bear to hear it, not yet. Not for a long time to come.'

'Then I'll just have to think up some other things you might like to hear,' he murmured. 'Like, "Yes, I'll accept your proposal." And if that runs out too soon, what about, "I love you" and "I think you're beautiful" and "I want you by my side for ever and always"?'

'Only that long?' Her face was alive with laughter as he yanked her down beside him. And against the dark strength of his throat, warm in the certainty and pure entitlement of his love, she breathed, 'Well, I suppose that will have to do for a start!'

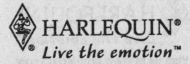

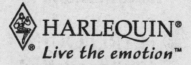

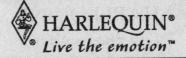

BETTY NEELS

Harlequin Romance® is proud to present this delightful story by Betty Neels. This wonderful novel is the climax of a unique career that saw Betty Neels become an international bestselling author, loved by millions of readers around the world.

A GOOD WIFE
(#3758)

Ivo van Doelen knew what he wanted—he simply needed to allow Serena Lightfoot time to come to the same conclusion. Now all he had to do was persuade Serena to accept his convenient proposal of marriage without her realizing he was already in love with her!

Don't miss this wonderful novel— brought to you by Harlequin Romance®!

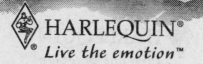

HARLEQUIN®
® *Live the emotion*™

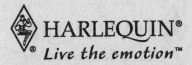

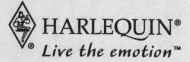

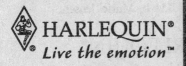
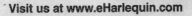

Harlequin Books presents

Forrester Square

LEGACIES . LIES . LOVE .

An exciting, new, 12-book continuity launching in August 2003.

Forrester Square…the elegant Seattle neighborhood where the Kinards, the Richardses and the Webbers lived… until one fateful night that tore these families apart.

Now, twenty years later, memories and secrets are about to be revealed as the children of these families are reunited. But one person is out to make sure they never remember….

Forrester Square… Legacies. Lies. Love.

Look for *Forrester Square,* launching in August 2003 with REINVENTING JULIA by Muriel Jensen.

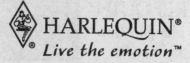